the
will

Smoke Over Shap

Smoke Over Shap

Margaret Potter

illustrated by Tony Morris

British Broadcasting Corporation

For My Mother

Smoke Over Shap was created for BBC children's programmes. It was first broadcast in six parts as a *4th Dimension* serial on Radio 4 in February 1974.

Published by the
British Broadcasting Corporation,
35 Marylebone High Street,
London W1M 4AA

ISBN 0 563 12762 7
First published 1975

Printed in England by Tonbridge Printers Ltd.

Chapter one

"To Cumberland? You want me to go to Cumberland?"

Joseph Locke, the famous railway engineer, smiled at the look of amazement on the face of his youngest assistant.

"How old are you now, Gerard?" he asked.

"I shall be twenty in a fortnight, sir."

"And you are still set on becoming a railway engineer?"

"I think you know I am."

"I should like to hear your reasons."

Gerard hesitated. This was his first interview with his employer since finishing his training. It was important to start off on the right footing.

"It is what my father would have wished, And . . . out of gratitude to you, sir, I feel –"

"Gratitude!" Mr Locke was obviously not impressed. "One does not choose the career of a lifetime out of gratitude! Besides you owe me none. Anything I have done for you has been out of my affection for your father. We were schoolboys together in Barnsley . . . grew up together . . . and chose the same profession. But for the grace of God, it could well have been me who perished in that rockfall at the Woodhead Tunnel!"

"I know that, sir. But I was going to say that, after the accident, when you took me into your own home, and paid for my education, I could not help but become interested in the building of the railways. Just hearing you talk about your work. It is an exciting job. And a challenging one. I honestly cannot think of anything I would rather do!"

"That's better! That's what I hoped to hear you say! It *is* exciting! The railways are changing the face of

Britain; bringing new ideas, new methods, to even the remotest parts of the country. And we are still only at the beginning! If this latest scheme goes through, in a few years' time we will be able to travel from London to Scotland in a matter of hours, instead of the days it takes at present!"

"You are referring to the Lancaster to Carlisle section of the Caledonian Railway, I take it, sir."

"I am, indeed! And this is why I have sent for you. Come over here."

Pushing back his chair, Mr Locke led the way to the far end of his office, where a huge coloured map covered one wall.

"This," he said, tapping the map with a forefinger, "this is the route I have already proposed to the Company. But, after going over the ground again just recently, I have been having second thoughts."

"You have discovered a better route, sir?"

"I believe so!"

Gerard considered the possibility. He knew just how important this scheme was to Mr Locke and the Railway Company he was working for. Already a competitor was building a line to Edinburgh along the East Coast. And there were some, particularly in Parliament, who considered that a second railway line into Scotland was not necessary. Yet to get to the rapidly-growing industrial city of Glasgow from London, a traveller still had to journey by rail to Liverpool, take a fourteen-hour sea journey to Ardrossan, and then a further rail journey into Glasgow. All this in the year 1843, when it took only eleven hours from London to Lancaster by rail!

The trouble was, of course, that the next section of the proposed line to Glasgow – between Lancaster and Carlisle – would have to travel across some of the most difficult terrain in the country – the mountainous region of Westmorland and Cumberland. And the hardest task of all would be to cross the bleak windswept wastes of Shap Fell! Joseph Locke had decided originally that the best way to overcome this obstacle was to tunnel beneath it – the tunnel to be a mile and a quarter long and reached by a line up the valley of the Lune through Kirby Lonsdale. But now it seemed he had other ideas.

"Tunnelling, as you know, my boy, is to be avoided wherever possible, on account of the cost. Also, this route takes us through the most sparsely populated part of the region." He paused, and producing a piece of charcoal from his pocket, started sketching a new thick black line upon the map. "Now, if we take our line nearer to Kendal, say to Oxenholme here, we shall serve the industry and population of that town. Then we swerve east to Grayrigg, on to Tebay, and then straight up and over Shap, and down into Penrith!"

Gerard gasped. "Did you say *over* Shap?"

Mr Locke chuckled. "I thought that would surprise you. I know Mr Stephenson says it cannot be done. But I say it can. And, by jove, if I can carry the Company with me, I am going to do it! And this is where you come in."

"M-me, sir?"

"Yes. There is a meeting of the Company shareholders in Kendal next week. I intend to put this plan before them. By then I'll need to have costs worked out down to the last farthing, and also to know just how long the operation will take – or as near as may be." He walked back to the desk again, Gerard following him in a daze.

Rummaging amongst the papers there, he drew out a thick leather-bound notebook, which had obviously seen a good deal of wear. Tossing it over to Gerard, he said: "These are my survey notes of the route, giving mileages, gradients, inclined planes, and so on. I want you to go over the ground and check every one of my figures – double-check if necessary. Then meet me at Kendal the day before the meeting, with your own report as to the feasibility of the plan! Think you can do it?"

His mind in a whirl, Gerard took a deep breath, and answered him straight. "Yes, sir! I know I can!"

"Humph!" Mr Locke's face was stern. "Well, we'll see. Till now it's all been theory. Here's your chance to put theory into practice. I'm relying upon you, Gerard. I need you, that notebook, and above all, your own views on the route . . . at Kendal, the day before the meeting!"

"I'll not let you down, sir!"

"See that you don't. And now, off with you. And good luck!"

Five days later Gerard was sitting in a stagecoach struggling over Shap Fell. A raging snowstorm blotted out the entire landscape. The wind howled and shrieked like a soul in torment. And in all the vast white wilderness, it seemed that nothing else lived or breathed. What little warmth there was inside the coach seemed to bring out the smell of mildewed leather and damp straw.

There were three other passengers besides Gerard. An elderly parson, and a young farmer and his wife, travelling from Penrith to Kendal.

Gerard thought the wife looked poorly. Her face was very pale, and she huddled in her corner seat, starting at every jolt and jerk the coach made as it slipped and swayed on the icy road.

Gerard shivered, and pulled his overcoat more closely around him. As he did so, he felt the bulky shape of the notebook in his inside pocket. He had completed his task, except for the report, which he would write as soon as he reached Kendal. Then he would be ready to face Mr Locke in the morning. This blizzard was alarming, though. He wondered how much further they had to go. He turned to the parson, nodding beside him.

"Where are we, do you suppose, sir?" he asked.

The parson straightened up, adjusting his wide-brimmed hat which had slipped a trifle to one side.

"My guess is that we are approaching the summit of Shap." He shuddered as a vicious gust of wind rattled the windows of the coach. " 'Pon my soul, I'd as soon ride out a storm at sea, as trust myself to these atrocious roads in midwinter!"

Gerard had to smile. "For myself, I'd have neither mode of transport. Give me a ride on smooth rails any day!"

"Ah!" The parson regarded him with interest. "You refer to the steam railway, I take it?"

"I do, sir!"

"And have you travelled much by this new-fangled railway?"

"A fair amount. Quite naturally so, since I am employed by Mr Joseph Locke. You have heard of him, of course?" Seeing the blank look on the parson's face, Gerard hastened to explain. "Mr Locke is the engineer responsible for the planning of the proposed Lancaster to Carlisle section of the new Caledonian Railway. He has built many railways up and down the country."

"I see." The parson looked suitably impressed. "And does that explain why you are travelling over Shap in midwinter when other, saner, mortals are safe at home?"

Gerard laughed. "It does."

"Well, then, Mister . . . . "

"My name is Gifford, Gerard Gifford. Your servant, sir!"

"Permit me to introduce myself then, Mr Gifford. I am the Reverend Josiah Linwood – parson of a small country parish near Tebay. Pray tell me, is it true that there is a possibility of the railway line being routed *over* Shap? Rumour has it so!"

Startled for a moment, Gerard paused. News travelled fast in this seemingly remote area. But after all, did it matter if he, or indeed Mr Locke, had been observed doing their survey, and conclusions drawn?

"Rumour for once, sir, is not at fault!"

"Then rumour be a jackass, I reckon!" The farmer opposite was glaring at him. His wife put out a restraining hand.

"Nay, Joady!" she said. "Tha knaws full well that an owd wife ower Lunesdale way foretells that carriages wi'out 'orses will one day run ower Loup Fell!"

The farmer sniffed. "Aye! She also says she can turn hersen into a hare – but theer's none seen 'er do it, as far as I con mek out!" He went on: "Even supposin' as the railway can be built – which I says as it can't – thee'll 'ave nowt but t'crows for passengers."

"Supposing I tell you that one day you farmers will be sending your cattle to market by rail – instead of walking the fat off them on the roads?"

"Come your railway," the farmer leaned forward angrily, "come your railway, an' we'll *'ave* no land, nor yet men to work it! Off to the towns they'll be for better wages nor we can pay 'em!"

Before Gerard had time to think of a reply, the coach gave a sudden lunge sideways, and the farmer's wife cried out in fright as they were thrown from their seats and on to the floor.

It took Gerard a moment to recover from the shock. Then, bracing his shoulders against the edge of the seat, he levered himself into a more or less upright position – though it was not easy as the coach was still tilted crazily on one side. His first thought was for the woman. She appeared to be buried beneath a pile of bundles and packages which had fallen from the rack above her head. Her husband lay beside her, dazed. Gerard grabbed him roughly by the shoulder, and shook him violently.

"Help me!" he cried. "Your wife!"

With a groan, the man struggled to his feet, and together they managed to extricate her. Cradling her in his arms, the farmer tried to calm her hysterical sobbing.

"Nay, nay, lass . . . thee's awreet, I tell 'ee! No harm done! Donna fret so!"

As Gerard turned to help the parson, who was also

struggling to regain his seat, the door of the coach opened, admitting a flurry of snow, and a cold blast of air. The woebegone face of the coachman, curiously foreshortened because of the angle of the coach, looked in.

"Trouble, folks!" it announced.

"We do not need to be told that!" Mr Linwood replied irritably, brushing straw off his gaiters. "What precisely is the extent of the damage?"

"We've lost a wheel! Off like a rocket, and half-way down t'fell by now! We'll be 'ere till daylight, so we mun mak the best on it!"

"We conna stay 'ere!" the farmer's wife sounded frantic. "We mun get on to Kendal! Tell 'em, Joady!"

There was a pause, then the farmer said, awkwardly: "She would come, gents. I did me best to put 'er off. But she's very near 'er time, d'you see."

"You mean she is with child?" Mr Linwood was shocked.

"Aye, sir. An' bein' 'er first, like, an' 'aving no other wimmin fowk at t'farm, we'm going to 'er sister at Kendal!"

"I see." Mr Linwood turned to the coachman. "If you took one of the horses, could you get through to Tebay, do you think?"

"Me?" Any other time the coachman's astonishment would have been comic. "Nay, parson, I'm not 'lowing to go nowhere till storm abates!" He turned on the farmer. "But yon's a ning-nang snafflen thing to do, is yon! What possessed you to bring her out in such a state – and on such a night?"

"Tis no conern o' thine! Thee'd do better gettin' after yon wheel, 'stead of yammerin' on at fowk!"

Gerard felt a tug at his sleeve. "Mek 'em stop, young sir," whispered the farmer's wife. She caught her breath and gave a pitiful little moan.

"I think one of us must go, sir," he said quietly to the parson. "We cannot expect her husband to leave her –

and if the coachman will not – "

"One can scarcely blame him! But you are right. I suggest we both go!"

Gerard was horrified. "I meant that I should go sir!"

"I am sure you did, and very commendable too. But consider. You are a stranger to these parts, whereas I have travelled the fells on horseback for more years than I care to remember." Mr Linwood smiled at the look of doubt on Gerard's face. "Come now, I am not as decrepit as all that! With my knowledge of the countryside, and your youthful enthusiasm to spur me on should the going get too difficult, I have no doubt we shall find our way to Tebay, and so send back help to these good people."

Reluctantly, seeing the sense of Mr Linwood's argument, Gerard gave in. Together they helped the coachman unharness two of the horses. Then, with a few comforting words to the farmer and his wife, they mounted, and set off on their mission.

As he watched the two figures disappearing into the distance, the coachman wondered whether he would ever see them *or* his horses again.

From where they left the coach, Mr Linwood reckoned it was about eight miles to Tebay, the nearest village. But to Gerard it seemed more like eighty as they battled their way through the storm. The wind drove the snow into their faces, where it stuck, freezing, clogging their eyelashes and nostrils, until every breath was agony and their vision was limited to a few yards. Sometimes they lost the road completely, and the horses, heavy beasts, floundered up to their bellies in drifts, and had to be manhandled out again, plunging and rearing with fright.

Gerard was amazed at the tenacity and courage of the parson, and at his extraordinary sense of direction. Time and again he was convinced that they were utterly lost, and on the point of giving up, only to hear Mr

Linwood's voice giving him confident commands to turn left or right, and then they would find themselves on the road again.

At last, however, a cluster of lights in the distance told them they had reached Tebay.

Once there, they made their way to the house of Doctor Graham, the local medical practitioner. They were lucky. He had only just returned from a sick call, yet when they told him their story, he turned out without

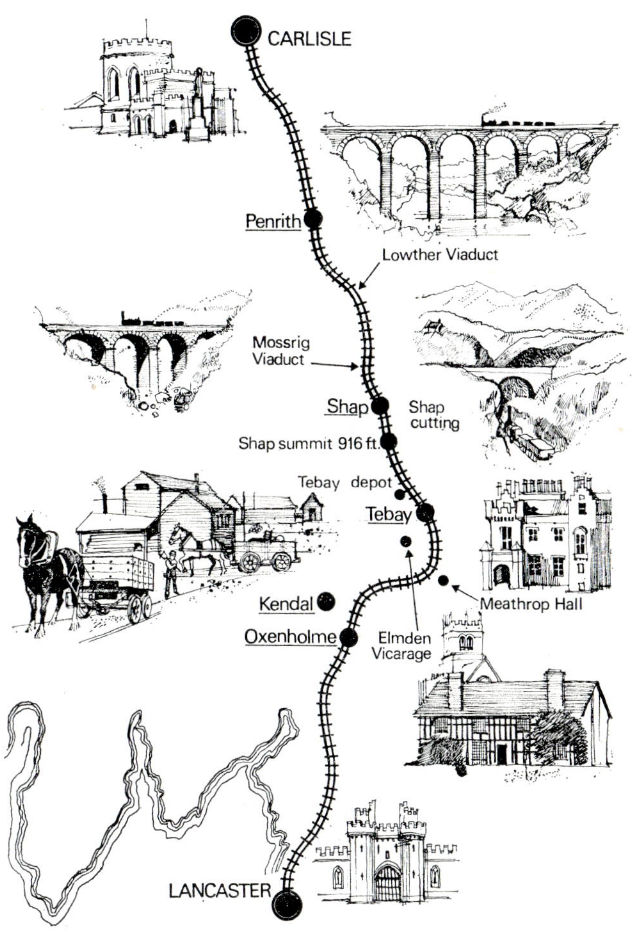

more ado, and set off in his gig in the direction from which they had come.

Their next call was upon the village wheelwright, a character named Meason, who gave them a somewhat surly reception. A few words from Mr Linwood, however, explaining the position, and he readily agreed to turn out with a new wheel for the stranded coach.

At last, their mission accomplished, they turned their weary horses towards Elmden Vicarage, Mr Linwood's home. Though the wind still raged furiously in gusts, the snow had stopped, and a pale moon shone intermittently through the clouds.

They were silent as they plodded on, too tired now for words. Gerard's mind was on the meeting with Mr Locke at Kendal the following day. He had no idea how far away Kendal was, or of the state of the roads between him and his destination. But he must get there in time, and with his report ready to hand over. Mr Locke was relying upon him, and he must not fail in this first task his benefactor had set him. Busy with his thoughts, he took no heed of where they were going, content to let his horse follow where Mr Linwood led.

Suddenly, the horse stopped beside a long low house ablaze with lights. The front door was open wide. And framed within it stood a slender red-haired girl in an emerald green gown.

"Father!" he heard her call. "Thank goodness you are safely home!"

Chapter two

A little while later, clad in dry clothes, and with a good meal inside him, Gerard was sitting in front of a roaring fire in the vicarage parlour, listening to Mr Linwood recounting their adventure.

His daughter, Bella, perched on a footstool at her father's feet, followed his every word with rapt attention. Not so the other occupant of the room, however, Bella's cousin, Ralph Rawlings.

He was a tall, rather bulky young man, about Gerard's own age. Dark of hair, and of complexion, he had a rather supercilious air about him. He listened listlessly to Mr Linwood's tale. But when the parson described how he had dispatched Meason, the wheelwright, to the stranded coach with a new wheel, Ralph was obviously annoyed.

"He'd not have done that for me, though I pay his wages! Idle fellow!"

"I think you are mistaken, Ralph," Mr Linwood protested. "Your father always said that he was one of his best men!"

Ralph shrugged. "My father, as you well know, sir, was too lenient with his work people!" He smiled arrogantly. "They know who is master now, though."

Bella turned hurriedly to Gerard. "You'll not mind a bed on the sofa in papa's study, Mr Gifford?"

Gerard explained that he must get on to Kendal, as he had an important meeting in the morning, and a report to write before then. But neither she nor Mr Linwood would hear of his leaving, so reluctantly he agreed to stay. He was determined, however, to set off at the crack of dawn next day.

Bella went to fetch blankets and pillows for his bed,

and Mr Linwood followed, saying it had been a very long day, and it was time to rest his old bones.

Gerard was about to follow them when Ralph stopped him abruptly: "A moment, Gifford! I want a word with you!"

Gerard hesitated. He was very tired, and there was still the report to write. Also, he had come to the conclusion that he did not much like Ralph Rawlings. But curiosity got the better of him, and he sat down again. Ralph's next remark, however, came as a considerable shock.

"This report of yours. Does it concern the route the new railway is to take between Tebay and Penrith?"

Gerard rose to his feet once more. "You really must excuse me . . . " he began.

"No! Wait! There is a reason for my asking. I have a vested interest at stake!"

Gerard shook his head. "I'm sorry, my information is confidential until the Company shareholders decide to release it! Have you land you wish to sell?"

Ralph laughed shortly. "On the contrary! I neither want nor intend to have your iron monsters snorting across *my* fields, terrifying my cattle, and setting fire to my crops!"

Gerard looked at him in amazement. "You are not serious?"

"I assure you I was never more so!"

Gerard laughed. "When people first saw Stephenson's 'Rocket' they thought it was the work of the Devil it's true! But that was twenty years ago. This is 1843! The railways are here to stay Mr Rawlings!"

"Maybe. But I own the largest estate in this area, Meathrop Hall. Twenty farms . . . forestry . . . saw mills . . . and some of the best arable land in the county. I am also the largest single employer of labour. Come your railway, and my workers will depart in quick sticks to work for the higher wages and shorter hours your

Company can afford to offer them. And, might I add, once they've left the land, they're not likely to return! *That* is why I am opposing your railway, Gifford!"

Gerard sighed. It was always the same. Progress halted by fear, suspicion, and hatred. No thought for the general good of the country, or, in this case, of what the railway would mean in terms of quick, safe, communication for a widely-scattered community.

"My company bring their own labour force with them, in the main," he began to explain, but Ralph cut him short.

"We know all about your work people. Your 'navvies', as you call them. A drunken thieving band of ruffians. The terror of ordinary decent folk!"

"There are good and bad amongst them like everyone else." Gerard was beginning to get angry. "But they are our responsibility. And we give fair compensation to anyone who suffers loss or damage through their actions. In any case, you cannot stop progress!"

"Can't I?" Ralph strode over to Bella's writing desk and sat down. "I am not the only one around here determined to see you and your railway company out of this district for good and all! Persist in your plans, and you'll have a fight on your hands!"

"You forget that the railway, when it comes, will be authorised by Act of Parliament! Are you proposing to oppose the law of the land?"

"If needs be. But it does not have to come to that! I have a proposition to put before you!" Pulling a sheet of paper from the rack, Ralph reached for a pen and began to write.

"Here is my draft for one hundred guineas, made out in your name, and payable on the day I hear your precious railway has by-passed my land!"

Anger left Gerard speechless. But only for a moment.

"I do not accept bribes! And you had better make up your mind to the fact that the railway will go through whichever route is decided upon! And, once we start, neither you, nor anybody else, is going to stop us! Goodnight, Mr Rawlings!"

The sofa in Mr Linwood's study had a screen around it, to keep out the draughts from the door, for the wind still howled and moaned outside. But although he was warm and comfortable, Gerard could not sleep. His mind was still going over the details of his report.

He had checked and double-checked all the information in Mr Locke's notebook, and the result was clear. The route over Shap was by far the more practical one. He would have no hesitation in confirming it on the next day.

Somewhere in the house a clock chimed, and then struck three. He turned over and composed himself for sleep. He slept. And yet he still seemed to be writing his report. The names of villages on the route unrolled before him in huge letters, white on black. He spelled them out . . . "Oxenholme and Greyrigg . . . Tebay and Bampton . . . Low Gill . . . Orton . . . Sleagill and Clifton." He heard the farmer's voice jeering: "Line over Shap! Thee'lt 'ave nowt but t'crows for passengers!" He saw Ralph's mocking smile as he offered him the bribe. And still in his dream, he sprang at him, knocking him to the ground. A chair turned over with a crash! Suddenly, Gerard was wide awake, his heart pounding against his ribs.

"Who's there?" he called.

He struggled out of his cocoon of blankets. The screen fell. In the silence which followed swift footsteps receded down the passage from his door.

Dawn was a ragged grey line on the horizon as Gerard left the house an hour or so later. He had written a note to Mr Linwood, thanking him for his hospitality, and the loan of a horse. As he approached the stable he was surprised to see a light in one of the windows. Pushing open the door, he went in and found Bella busy harnessing a chestnut mare. Turning, she laughed at his look of astonishment.

"Good morning! You are in luck. The road to Kendal is fairly clear. Apparently the worst of the snow was north of here. So you should have no trouble in keeping your appointment. Besides, I am lending you my mare, Maria. She goes like a bird, providing you talk sweetly to her!"

"I . . . I shall be for ever in your debt!" Gerard stammered.

"Nonsense! The exercise will do her good! And if you leave her with the ostler at the King's Head, she will be in good hands. Papa will drive me in to fetch her back tomorrow."

"She certainly is a beauty!"

"You should just see her racing up the fells on a fine day! With the clouds flying . . . and the curlews calling! It's as if she had wings! Maggie says days like that iron the creases out of my soul!"

"Maggie?"

"The housekeeper. Oh, I forgot. She was in bed by the time you came home last night!"

"And *do* you have creases in your soul?"

She made a face at him. "Sometimes! This place is so dull! Nothing ever happens. Nothing *vital*, that is. Do you know what I mean?"

"I think so. People our age need to be in the thick of things. *Doing* rather than just *being*! At least . . . I do. Does that sound pompous?"

"No! That's exactly how I feel! I want to do something important with my life!"

But Gerard's attention was suddenly distracted. "How odd!"

"What are you looking at?"

He bent down and picked something up out of the straw.

"What is it?"

"It's my notebook!" He was puzzled. "I saw a corner of it sticking out of the straw by my foot!"

"You must have dropped it when you brought the horses in last night!"

"But I couldn't possibly – " Gerard stopped. It was no use embarking on a long explanation. A thought occurred to him, however. "By the way, I have left a note for your father, thanking him for his great kindness, but perhaps you will say goodbye to your cousin Ralph for me?"

"Oh, Ralph's gone. He left very early. Long before I was up. And that *is* odd! He hates getting up early!"

"Does he? I fancy he takes the running of his estate very seriously."

Bella sighed. "I suppose so. Yet I sometimes wonder." She paused, then went on, "Before his father died last year, Ralph was scarcely ever up here. He was always in London, or Bath . . . or Brighton. Anywhere he could find boon companions and a gaming table!" She stopped and put her hands over her mouth. "There! Papa's quite right! I am always letting my tongue run away with me!"

Gerard laughed. "Does your cousin also find country life dull, then?"

"Oh, he contrives to keep himself amused! He has his little coterie of friends, with like interests. They've formed themselves into a club of sorts. The Chanticleers! Their headquarters are at Meathrop Hall.

"Why 'Chanticleers'?"

There was a note of disgust in Bella's voice. "Cock fighting as a sport is still very much in vogue hereabouts. London does not have the monopoly of cruelty and vice!" Abruptly she finished: "Sometimes I wish that cousin Ralph had stayed in the south!"

Gerard felt suddenly very sorry for her. "Miss Linwood," he began.

She smiled. "My friends call me Bella!"

"All right then . . . Bella. What I wanted to say . . . to ask you . . . well, that is . . . may I write to you sometimes?"

Eagerly, Bella replied. "Would you? And tell me all about your work? I'd like that very much!"

"You would not find it . . . dull?"

"How could it be? Father says the railway will be a boon and a blessing to us all! I'm sure he is right, whatever cousin Ralph may say!" She hesitated, then said shyly: "And may I write to you, too? Can you bear the ramblings of a country mouse?"

"Of course. And my name is Gerard!"

"Very well, Gerard. I shall look forward to your letters! And now you must be on your way. I hope you have a safe journey to Kendal."

Chapter three

Later that same morning, an unexpected visitor awaited Ralph Rawlings in the library of Meathrop Hall. He was a sallow-complexioned little man, with sharp, inquisitive eyes, and a furtive foxy air about him. As he waited, he consulted a rather grubby pile of papers which he had taken from his coat pocket. Every now and then, however, he would look up, and gaze thoughtfully around, as if mentally costing the books, the furnishings, and the fine pictures which the room contained.

Ralph, when he came in, was in a hurry and in no very amiable mood. He held the man's visiting card between thumb and forefinger.

"Mr Nathan Raphael?" he barked.

The little man bowed in assent.

"I see you represent Raphael, Hunt and Palmer of Slack Lane, York. But your card does not state your business!" He eyed the man disdainfully, noting his dingy grey suit and soiled neckcloth.

Raphael smiled. "As to that, sir, it is of a somewhat confidential nature, and I find it . . . shall we say more discreet . . . to leave such details undisclosed. In print, at any rate."

Ralph seated himself at the desk. "I am extremely busy, Mr Raphael," he began. "So perhaps you will kindly come to the point?"

"Certainly, sir. With the greatest of pleasure. I am here on behalf of a client. M'Lord Eskdale, to be exact!"

"Eskdale!"

"Dear me, Mr Rawlings! Are you not feeling well? You have suddenly grown very pale."

"So! You are a debt collector, is that it?"

"I am an emissary from that noble gentleman, yes!

I have here a document which concerns you!" Raphael fumbled in an inside pocket, and produced a folded piece of paper, which he placed upon the desk.

Ralph waved it away. "There is no need to show it to me! I know what it is! An I.O.U. I gave Eskdale for five hundred guineas. It was due to be redeemed six weeks ago. Well! He is out of luck! For I've not got it, nor anything like that amount!"

"Dear me!" Raphael contemplated the tip of a rather muddy shoe. "That is most inconvenient! Most!"

"That is to say," Ralph went on hurriedly, "that is to say, that I have not got it *at the moment*! M'Lord Eskdale will give me time to settle, surely?"

"I am rather afraid not!"

"But he must! When I signed that I.O.U., my father had just died and I fully expected to inherit the estate right away! Then I found it had been left in trust until I am twenty-three, in two years' time. Until then, I cannot touch a penny of the capital!"

Raphael sighed. "It is very vexing for you, I am sure, Mr Rawlings. However . . . I am afraid . . . " He shrugged his shoulders.

"But there is nothing I can do about it!" Ralph sounded desperate. "My mother, as my appointed guardian, keeps tight hold of the purse strings. If she knew I had run up gambling debts to the tune of five hundred guineas, there'd be the very dickens of a row! Surely, if you explain to Lord Eskdale that it is not a question of my defaulting, but merely needing more time!"

"H'm!" Taking a small box from his waistcoat, Raphael helped himself to a liberal pinch of snuff, thereby adding greatly to the stains already decorating that article of clothing.

"It may very well be that a way could be . . . could be . . . " He sneezed so violently Ralph thought his head must surely leave his shoulders.

"Well?" he said impatiently.

The little man trumpeted into a large red bandanna handkerchief, and then sighed with relief. "Ah! That's better! As I was saying Mr Rawlings. I think there may well be a way out of your present . . . difficulty! You may, or you may not know that his Lordship is a shareholder in the company financing the East Coast railway route to Scotland."

"No, I did not know!"

"Well, as a shareholder of the Company, his Lordship views, with considerable alarm, the prospect of a rival route, via the West Coast. You do see his point?"

"Of course! Why share the passengers and profits between two lines when one would suffice?"

"Exactly, sir!" For the first time the hint of a wintry smile briefly crossed Raphael's face. "I believe it is going to be a pleasure to do business with you after all!"

"Business? What sort of business?"

Raphael glanced over his shoulder, as if to assure himself that they were alone, then leaned forward confidentially. "His Lordship was most explicit. In the event of your being unable to settle your debt immediately, I was to tell you that he might forgo the matter entirely on certain conditions!"

"You mean . . . I would not have to pay back the money?"

"Precisely!"

"But that is marvellous! What are the conditions his Lordship requires?"

"Firstly, you must try to 'discourage' the West Coast route by every means at your disposal!"

Ralph laughed. "My dear sir! I am already determined that the railway, if it comes, will not cross *my* land!"

"Good, good. We . . . er . . . we had already ascertained your feelings on this point. But, supposing the Government gives permission for the West Coast route to be built? Would you be prepared to devise ways and means to ensure that it never reaches Carlisle? Or at least, does not get there until after we – that is, the East Coast Company, have already completed our line to Edinburgh."

"I beg your pardon!"

"I see I have shocked you, Mr Rawlings. His Lordship has invested a considerable fortune in the East Coast route, along with Mr George Hudson and others. He is not prepared to see his interests . . . jeopardised!"

"I can understand that! But do you realise what you are implying? Why, it is . . . it is tantamount to sabotage!"

"It is best not to put labels on things, in my view, Mr Rawlings. I am sure you will agree!"

Ralph was silent. He felt helpless. Trapped. And he realised that the trap was of his own making.

He looked at the I.O.U. lying on the desk. It needed but a split second to snatch it up and destroy it. Then his troubles would be over, and there would be no need to make a decision. But even as the thought came to him, Raphael stretched out a hand, and calmly pocketed the wretched document once more.

"Well, sir? And what am I to tell his Lordship?"

There was a little pause. Then Ralph rose to his feet, and walked to the door. "My compliments to Lord Eskdale. You may tell him that he can count on my co-operation!"

The meeting of the shareholders of the Lancaster and Carlisle Railway in Kendal had been in progress for nearly four hours.

Gerard's jaws ached with the effort to conceal his yawns. He was very tired. He supposed it was reaction to the events of the past twenty-four hours. Joseph Locke had been pleased with his report. Not only because it concurred with his own views, but because, as he said,

"It was a thoroughly workmanlike job!" But now the long-winded speeches, and the overheated room were making him sleepy. As yet another worthy rose to address the meeting, Gerard made an effort to pull himself together, and asked Mr Locke who it was.

"That, my boy," said Mr Locke with a chuckle, "that is Cornelius Nicholson, the Mayor of Kendal. And you may be sure he'll be for the new route! He owns the paper mill at Burneside – the biggest industry in the town, I should think!"

But Mr Nicholson was already being heckled by a short, very red-faced gentleman in rough tweeds.

"Sir!" he was saying. "The route proposed in the first place, is shorter by about a mile and a quarter than the new route proposed by Mr Locke. It would also cost approximately thirty-six thousand pounds *less* to build! Why then should we consider the new one at all?"

There were murmurs of agreement all round the table. But Cornelius Nicholson would not be put off. Pounding the table with his fist he cried: "I will give you my answer to that, sir! We must consider the new route for one very excellent reason! It would serve this town of ours, a thriving industrial town, which contains the greatest concentration of population in the area. No less than nine thousand souls, at the last count."

He glared furiously at the red-faced man and then sat down.

The hubbub broke out again, and this time it was the chairman who banged his gavel on the table, bringing the meeting to order. "Gentlemen," he pleaded, "we shall get nowhere at this rate!"

Joseph Locke jumped to his feet. "If I may be permitted to address the meeting once again, Mr Chairman, I think I may be able to clarify one or two points which still seem to be in doubt."

With a sigh of relief, the chairman sat down and Joseph Locke took the floor.

"It is true," he began, "that the route originally surveyed and proposed for the line would be a mile and a quarter shorter, easier from the engineering point of view, and would cost thirty-six thousand pounds less than the new route I have laid before you. But a great many people object to it. For two main reasons. The first is that it would cut through the Lune Valley, one of the most beautiful and fertile areas in the county, and, in so doing, would destroy the amenities of many private properties. Secondly, it would only serve a comparatively small population. Whereas the new route, as Mr Nicholson has so rightly observed, would cater for the people and industry of Kendal, a rapidly expanding industrial town. As to the objection to taking the line over Shap, which, you may take my word for it, gentlemen, *can* be done . . . we would save not only a further mile between Tebay and Penrith, but also the cost of having to tunnel under Orton Scar. A cost which would be in the region of a hundred and forty thousand pounds!"

There was a buzz of excitement around the table, but Locke went on: "The fact of the matter is, gentlemen, that I am so convinced that this latter route is the best possible one for the line to take, that if it is adopted, I will give the Company my personal guarantee that the whole seventy miles of track, with its accompanying fifteen turnpike road bridges . . . sixty-four public road bridges . . . and eighty-six occupation bridges . . . will be completed within *two years* of the day on which the first sod is cut!"

There was a moment of stunned silence, and then Locke resumed his seat to a buzz of excited talk.

"I think you've won your case sir!" said Gerard. "Even our friend in the tweeds is looking interested!"

Joseph Locke beamed. "It looks promising – very promising. By the way, what are you doing this evening, after we've finished here?"

"Nothing particular, sir. Except that I had planned to write a letter!"

"Stay and have a bite of supper with me first. I've something I want to discuss with you!"

"I'll be glad to, sir!"

"Good. I have an errand for you tomorrow!"

Joseph Locke was in excellent spirits during supper. He was confident that he had persuaded the Company to support the new route over Shap. Most of the money for the venture had already been subscribed. As far as he was concerned, the Caledonian Railway – Section One (Lancaster to Carlisle) was already in business. Now he was anxious to start the preliminary work of organising supplies and labour. After they had finished eating, he lit up a pipe, settled back in his chair and looked across at Gerard.

"I would like you to stay up here, for the time being, my boy," he said. "I have other commitments and need to be free to come and go as I please. But I must have someone here to act as my go-between with all the various people concerned. The contractors, sub-contractors, local landowners, and the like. Think you can handle it?"

"I think so, sir!" Gerard was excited at the prospect.

"People will say you're too young for the responsibility, of course!"

"That is up to you to decide, surely?"

Joseph Locke laughed.

"Besides," Gerard went on eagerly. "I've got to know the area quite well these last few days, under the worst possible conditions. And I *have* made one or two useful contacts. The Reverend Linwood, for example. He is really enthusiastic about the coming of the railway. I know I can count on his help if there's any trouble!"

He had told Joseph Locke about his adventures on Shap but had not mentioned his conversation with Ralph Rawlings.

"Ah yes, Mr Linwood!" Locke smiled. "You said he

had a charming daughter too, I think! About your own age. Does she share his enthusiasm?"

Gerard was annoyed to feel himself colouring. He wished he had not mentioned Bella. Still, if he was going to stay in the area for a while, it was nice to think he might see her sometimes. He intended to write to her before going to bed, so that she might know of his safe arrival in Kendal.

But Locke was speaking again. "However, you'll not be left to your own devices entirely. Now, about tomorrow. I think I mentioned I had an errand for you!"

"Yes, sir?"

"I want you to go to Lancaster to see Mr Brassey for me!"

"Mr Brassey!"

"There's no need to look so apprehensive. He's not likely to eat you!"

Gerard thought of all he'd heard about Thomas Brassey – the most powerful railway contractor in the country. He controlled a vast army of navvies, thousands of them. He had already built hundreds of miles of railways here in England and had just finished the first continental railway – from Paris to Rouen. It was said that if ever Thomas Brassey went bankrupt (not that he was ever likely to), the unemployment rate in the country would immediately rise by one per cent. Brassey had a genius for organisation on a large scale. He was known as a good and just employer. Thomas Brassey and Joseph Locke had worked together on many projects. Gerard had never met him. And it was Brassey who would be in charge of the actual building of the new line.

"As you know," Locke went on, "we are at present working on what will eventually be the link-up between the Preston to Lancaster Junction, and the Lancaster/Carlisle line. Mr Brassey is in Lancaster now, supervising the work. I want him to have a résumé of today's meeting, Gerard, and also my observations on some of the difficulties we are likely to encounter once we get the go-ahead from Parliament. It is all written down here."

He handed Gerard a large flat envelope.

"You had better make an early start in the morning. You'll have no trouble in finding the workings – anybody in Lancaster will be able to direct you to them. But don't be surprised if you have to go looking for Mr Brassey along the line! He's not one for sitting in an office. And wear some good stout boots!"

Joseph Locke laughed at the expression on his young assistant's face. "I don't expect you to *walk* to Lancaster! But you'll need them once you get there, I promise you!"

As it turned out, once he arrived at the workings, Gerard had no trouble in finding Brassey. A workman directed him to a small wooden hut at the side of the track. He knocked, and a pleasant, well-modulated voice told him to enter.

The hut was furnished with a chair, a trestle table, and a canvas folding bed in a corner. Beside the table stood Thomas Brassey. He was much younger than Gerard had imagined, not more than forty. His thick mop of hair was greying, and he had a roundish, weatherbeaten, good-humoured face. He greeted Gerard courteously, and taking the package which Mr Locke had sent, waved Gerard to the chair, while he went over to the window to study its contents. When he had finished, he came back. Perching himself on a corner of the table, he subjected Gerard to a sharp scrutiny.

"So!" he said, at last. "Mr Locke has condescended to loan me the services of his boy wonder!"

Gerard was furious. "Sir!" he began, "I – I – "

Brassey laughed. "No offence meant, Gifford," he said. "But I'm not used to having an assistant! Away from my London office I have always been my own amanuensis. Indeed, I shall let you into a secret."

He paused, and then crossed to the window again. He stared out for a few moments, then turning back, went on: "Most of my calculations in the field are done on backs of envelopes, bills or any other scraps of paper I may have about me. Tell me, do you walk?"

Gerard stared at him. "I had much rather ride!"

"Whilst you are with me, you will walk! Mile upon mile . . . over mountains and moorlands, through streams, aye, and rivers even, should the necessity arise. Does the prospect alarm you?"

"No, sir. I am just a little surprised . . . "

"You thought I would travel everywhere by coach . . . or on horseback, staying only at the best inns and hostelries? I am sorry to disappoint you. But that is the way I inspect the work in progress on any job I have contracted to build. On foot – so that nothing, not the smallest, the most insignificant detail, escapes my eye! The men are accustomed to seeing me, and they work the better for it!"

"Yes, sir!"

"It is to be the Shap route, then, eh?"

"It seems so, sir!"

"It will be a challenge! Think of it, Gifford. Four miles to the summit. A rise of 1,000 feet, and a gradient of one in seventy-five!"

"It's wild country, sir. I know from personal experience. I was travelling over Shap but two days ago, in a blizzard, and the coach lost a wheel."

"Then you know what we are up against. I warn you, you will have to rough it alongside the navvies. No feather beds in cosy inns. A wooden shack such as this, beside the track. With a roof that leaks, and if you're in luck, a bed of bracken!"

Gerard couldn't help himself. He laughed outright at the picture Brassey drew for his benefit. And Brassey laughed, too.

"Your father was a railway engineer, was he not?

Killed in a rock fall at Woodhead? I remember Mr Locke telling me about him. Well, he says your heart and soul is in the railways, too. And that's what I like to hear. We shall get on very well, Gifford, I have no doubt!"

There was a sudden shout of alarm outside . . . and the rattle of a wagon approaching at speed. Brassey was at the door and out of it in a matter of seconds, and Gerard followed. Down the line towards them rolled a flat wagon piled high with wooden sleepers. Directly in its path stood a labourer with a barrow straddled across the line.

"Clear the track!" roared Brassey. "You there, with the barrow! Move yourself!"

"He doesn't hear you!" shouted Gerard, horrified, and leapt forward.

"Gifford! Come back!" shouted Brassey. The other workers stood rooted to the spot, watching the flying figure.

Gerard reached the labourer, and literally threw him to one side just as the wagon hit the barrow with a crash, splintering it into a thousand pieces. It rolled on until it hit another wagon which was being unloaded further down the track. There was a second crash, and sleepers exploded into the air like so many matchsticks. The wagon itself upended, and then fell with a noise like thunder!

"Are you all right, lad?" Brassey bent over Gerard, where he and the man with the barrow lay, winded, after the impact of Gerard's flying tackle.

"Yes, I'm all right!" said Gerard, getting to his feet.

The labourer also struggled to his feet. "I couldna' shift barrow one road or t'other!" he mumbled.

"Then you should have had the sense to leave it," said Brassey curtly. He turned and stalked off shouting, "Now then, you men, no use standing around gawping! Get those sleepers cleared up and get the wagon back on the track! Come along now."

Gerard went back into the hut, and sat down. His legs were shaking, and he'd hurt a knee when he'd crashed to the ground. But a second later he heard Brassey calling his name, and he hobbled out again.

"Over here!" Brassey was standing beside the upturned wagon. "Take a look at this," he said quietly, as Gerard came up to him.

He pointed to one of the wheels, which was still spinning from the force of the impact. "You see what's happened? The handle of the ratchet on the brake mechanism? It's been sawn off!"

Gerard gasped. "You mean – "

"Yes, deliberately. At least, it looks very much like it. If you ask me, boy, we'll have more than the elements to contend with before we see smoke over Shap!"

Chapter four

Two weeks later Gerard was busy checking lists of stores at one of the main assembly depots – a large hutted encampment near Tebay – when a reporter from the *Westmorland Gazette* asked if he could have a word with him. Thomas Brassey had warned Gerard to expect this visit, and told him to be as diplomatic as possible. Now that the railway was seen to be a reality, feeling in the area was running high.

The increased traffic on the narrow country roads and lanes was one of the chief causes of trouble. The roads between Lancaster and Kendal were at times in a state of complete chaos, with wagon loads of timber and iron rails competing with farm carts and wagonettes for right of way.

The assembly depot was a scene of bustling activity. While some wagons were being rapidly unloaded, empty ones were driven away, and huge piles of boxes and barrels were being carted into sheds. Over everything was a rumble of heavy wheels, a clanging and clatter from tools and equipment being sorted, and men shouting. The noise was indescribable.

"Confusion worse confounded, I see," the reporter remarked, as he looked around. "The name's Bishop, by the way. George Bishop!"

Gerard smiled. "Well, Mr Bishop. It will be different in a day or two, when we are better organised!"

"Still, it's nothing to the chaos on the roads! Had many complaints about it from the locals?"

"A few. But I've told them it's only a temporary nuisance. Excuse me a moment." A short, thickset man, with reddish hair and a ruddy complexion had come up and was waiting to speak to him. "What is it, Jake?"

Jake Joynson, the chief overseer, jerked a thumb over his shoulder. "Powder wagon's just in from Gatebeck, Mr Gifford!"

Gerard turned as a long wagon, pulled by a team of six horses, came rumbling towards him. The wagon was piled high with wooden barrels securely roped together.

Gerard checked his list. "There should be fifty barrels there. Have you checked them?"

"Aye."

"Good. You know which shed they're to go in. Get some of the men to help you unhitch the horses, and roll the wagon inside. Then padlock the door and bring me the key!"

"Right you are!" Jake turned away shouting: "All right, Joe! Follow me!"

The driver gave a nod, and the wagon lumbered off, following the overseer's sturdy figure as he strode towards a group of large wooden buildings on the outer perimeter of the depot.

"Gunpowder, is it?" the reporter gave a low whistle. "Enough for a mighty big bang!"

"Enough to blast through several thousand tons of rock!"

"Bit dangerous don't you think? Storing it all in one place?"

"It's only here for the night, Mr Bishop. Tomorrow it will be moved up to Shap!"

"Folks round here are betting you'll never lay a line across Shap!"

"Our engineer, Mr Locke, is confident we shall!"

"You must admit though, that Shap's a daunting proposition. Man, it's like the roof of the world up there! You've not only got the hard whinstone rock to contend with. There'll be snow, ice, and winds that freeze the very marrow in your bones." The reporter laughed, then went on. "You propose tackling all that with a rabble of rogues and vagabonds – armed with picks and shovels?"

The reporter glanced around with a pitying smile. Gerard felt his temper beginning to rise. But, remembering Brassey's instructions, he resolved to be patient. "Have you ever seen a railway being built, Mr Bishop?" Gerard asked.

"No more I have," was the answer.

"Then perhaps you'd let me explain how we tackle a job like the laying of the line across Shap Fell, for instance!"

"Surely!" Bishop produced notebook and pencil from a pocket, "Mind if I take notes?"

"Not at all. If you don't mind standing out here. I like to be on the spot in case any queries come up."

"Go right ahead. It suits me fine."

Gerard sighed with relief. At least if he got the fellow interested in the actual building operation, he might keep off more controversial topics.

"Well," he began, "in the first place, when we make a cutting, which is what we'll be doing across Shap, it won't be with any 'rabble of rogues and vagabonds'. It'll be with an army of five hundred experienced navigators, or 'navvies', as we call them. Some of the toughest and strongest working men in the world!"

Bishop looked up from his scribbling, and grinned. "I take your point," he said.

Gerard smiled. "Actually it's a bit like cutting a wedge out of a cake, I suppose. Except that we have to mark out the line of the 'cut' over the top of the hill, so that the men have a guide to work to. We do this with posts and rails. Then the top soil is dug out and carted away so that gradually the hill is laid open, and a gully formed."

Gerard paused. He could see that the reporter was getting interested. He went on to describe how a temporary light rail was laid in the gulley for horses to draw trains of wagons alongside the navvies, who were working on the slopes above.

"Each wagon," he explained, "is filled by two men

working together, shovelling the muck – that's what we call the loose earth and stones which lie on the surface – over their heads and into the wagon below!"

"How much muck can a man shift in a day?"

"Twenty tons is the average!"

"Twenty tons!" Bishop was staggered. "Go on, Mr Gifford. This information will interest our readers."

"Well, then, with the navvies working either side of the track, filling the wagons, and another party working on ahead to extend the gully, the work proceeds. When we come to rock, we blast it out of the way. And the loose stone which the explosion displaces is used to build bridges, to fill in, or to strengthen bankings."

"Could be an element of danger in the work, I suppose?"

"Yes, indeed. Especially when we reach the bottom of the cutting. At Shap Fell, by the time we reach bottom, we'll be sixty feet down – and we'll have to lift the muck up all of that sixty feet to dump it at the top. It can be very dangerous, then, when the men are making the running!"

Noting the reporter's puzzled expression, Gerard went on to explain what the term "making the running" meant. He described how planks were laid from the top to the bottom of the cutting to form a narrow staging just wide enough for a man to wheel a barrow up it. The navvies filled the barrow with the muck, then a rope was attached to the barrow and to the navvy's waist belt. The rope ran up the staging and over a pulley wheel at the top, where it was attached to a horse. When the barrow was full a signal was given to the horse minder, and the horse walked round pulling on the rope so that the navvy was drawn up the plank balancing the barrow in front of him.

"Why couldn't you use tubs instead of barrows?" the reporter wanted to know.

"Because the angle's far too steep. Tubs would just

bounce and spill."

"But supposing the horse stops, and the rope goes slack?"

"Then the barrow and its contents are likely to fall on top of the man, and they both go plummeting down to the bottom!"

"Does it often happen?"

"More often than we like. As I said, it can be very dangerous, especially in wet weather!"

Bishop scribbled industriously for a moment or two, then looked up again.

"Two more questions, Mr Gifford. How does the navvy get to the bottom of the cutting again?"

"After he's tipped the muck at the top, he turns round, and goes back down the plank, this time drawing the barrow *behind* him. Again, it is up to the horse to keep the rope taut and so take the weight of the barrow and that of the navvy."

"One more point. What are they paid for this sort of work? If you can call it work. More like hard labour!"

"About seventeen shillings a week. Most of which goes on food . . . and beer. Two loaves of bread, two pounds of beef, and five quarts of beer. That's their usual daily ration!"

"Well, they earn it!" Bishop finished writing and closed his notebook with a snap. "It's the beer that causes the trouble though, isn't it?"

Gerard groaned inwardly. He knew what was in the reporter's mind. Best let him get it off his chest. "What trouble, Mr Bishop?"

"Oh come now! You know what I mean. There have been twenty convictions for robbery with violence in Kendal this past month. All navvies. To say nothing of crops being trampled, henhouses raided, and brawls galore. Once the drink's in, these navvies of yours are more like wild animals than human beings!"

"They're hard men, doing a hard job! Be fair, Mr

Bishop! You had crime here before we came on the scene!"

"But not on this scale! I tell you, the farmers are talking of raising a vigilante committee to protect their property!"

"They've a perfect right to do so, of course." Gerard tried to speak reasonably. It would do no good to antagonise this man. "Once we get the line started we will, in any case, be employing our own police force to maintain law and order." He went on, "I know Mister Brassey would be obliged if you could see your way to making a special note of that in your newspaper article."

Bishop nodded. "You can count on it, Mr Gifford. But I think it only fair to warn you, if they have much more provocation, the farmers are likely to take matters into their own hands." He smiled, and held out his hand. "It's been a pleasure talking to you. I'll see you get a copy of my article when it appears. I'll not take up any more of your time. Good day!"

Gerard watched him depart, threading his way through the maze of men, horses, wagons, and equipment. In his mind's eye he had a picture of a horde of angry farmers carrying flails and pitchforks confronting a gang of navvies armed with picks and shovels. Fear, like a trickle of icy water, crept down his spine. He took up the check list he had been working on when the reporter interrupted him, and tried to lose his thoughts in work.

Later, as it was getting dusk, Jake Joynson came to the hut which served Gerard as office. It was small and dark, sparsely furnished with a scrubbed wooden table and plain kitchen chair. In one corner, beneath a row of nails which served as files for papers, a camp bed had been set up, with blankets neatly folded upon it.

Gerard looked up from his writing as Jake came in.

"I've brought the keys, sir!"

Jake placed them on the table. "The oil store . . . lamp shed . . . and this one's off the padlock on the powder shed."

"Thanks," Gerard reached over, and pocketed the latter.

Jake looked at the bed, and at Gerard's valise standing at the foot of it. He cleared his throat. "Thinkin' of sleepin' here tonight, Mr Gifford?"

Gerard stretched his arms above his head, trying to get rid of the cramp in his fingers. "I am, as a matter of fact, Jake. While the gunpowder's on the site. In any case, I've some writing to do. Lists of stores still to come."

"Aye, well . . . in that case," Jake turned and went out of the hut, but was back in seconds, carrying a shotgun.

"If you're bent on staying," he said, "I might as well leave this!" He leaned it against the table.

Gerard burst out laughing. "What on earth would I do with that?"

"Might feel like potting something . . . say a rabbit or two in the morning. Mr Brassey borrows it when he sleeps on the site."

"Oh does he? Well, leave it then. Put it over there in the corner."

Jake did as he was told, and came back to the table. He seemed loath to leave. "Known Mr Brassey for long, sir?"

"No."

"He's a one is Mr Brassey," Jake chuckled. "Ten years since I first clapt eye on 'im. On the Grand Junction. I mind one of the navvies – a strapping big feller from Cork – saying to me 'Sure an' if Mr Brassey had been a parson, he'd 'ave been a bishop! An' if he'd been a prize fighter, he'd have won the Belt, so 'e would'!"

They both laughed, and Gerard suddenly felt more relaxed. Bluff, tough, and honest, there was something very reassuring about Jake. And not easily riled, as Gerard had had opportunity to find out these last few days.

"He certainly is a remarkable man, Jake. He's some very advanced notions about the welfare of his navvies.

D'you know he's thinking of building a chapel and a school for them, at Shap?"

"Aye, well, they'll need summat to keep 'em out of mischief up there. Else the Irish'll fight the Scots, and the English'll fight the both of them – just to relieve the monotony!"

"By the way, I meant to ask you about this earlier on," Gerard picked up a letter from the table. "There's a chap called Turnbull coming to see me tomorrow. He wants a permit to sell beer to the men. Is it all above board?"

"Oh, aye, Turnbull's as straight as a die! We've dealt with him before."

"Right!" Gerard scribbled on the letter and put it aside. "Can't help thinking though, Jake, that it would be a blessing if we could ban it altogether. I've watched some of them drinking in the grog shop on pay night, and they scarcely seem human at all. It's what that reporter from the *Gazette* was saying too."

"They're what life's made 'em Mr Gifford. If you don't mind my saying so, you're very young to have such responsibility. And new to the game. Can I give you a piece of advice?"

"By all means!"

"Well, if you ever meet up with any trouble amongst the navvies . . . face 'em! Don't turn your back on 'em! Not until you've got the upper hand, that is!"

"Even at the risk of being knocked down?"

"Better that than a knife between your shoulder blades! Shocks you, doesn't it? But I've seen it happen – more than once!"

It was there again. That icy chill down his spine. Gerard took a deep breath. "Thanks, Jake. I'll remember what you say!"

"Right, then I'm off! Good night!"

As the door closed behind him, Gerard took up his pen again. But after a few minutes he pushed aside the lists of stores he had been working on, and reached for a piece of writing paper. He would write to Bella. He owed her a letter, in any case. He felt a sudden longing for contact with a safe and civilised world, far removed from his present surroundings.

Chapter five

Recently Bella had taken to walking down to meet the mail cart which usually arrived about midday. Today, as it turned into the lane leading to the vicarage she wondered whether there would be a letter from Gerard. Jonty, the carrier, cum-postman, cum-village handyman, called out a cheery greeting as he drew up beside her. But she was due to be disappointed.

"None for you today, Miss Bella! All for parson – mainly bills, by the looks of 'em!"

"All right Jonty!" She smiled as she took the pile of letters from him. "How is the baby?"

"She'm comin' along champion, Miss." Jonty's face fair beamed at the thought of his newest small daughter. "Wife's plannin' to see parson soon about christenin'."

"Oh, good." Bella turned and retraced her steps to the vicarage. In the hall she met her father preparing to go out.

"I've several visits to make, Bella, my dear," he said, taking the letters from her. "In particular, I want to call at Bellamy's, so I shan't be back until about six at the very earliest. Don't wait tea for me, I expect I'll have had my fill of tea and scones by the time I get back!"

He glanced through the letters, and tossed them on to the hall table.

"There's nothing there that can't wait. What about you? Did you hear from Gerard?"

"No," Bella replied with a sigh. "I expect he's too busy for letter writing."

"I expect so," Mr Linwood said gravely, but with a twinkle in his eye.

Bella looked at him and laughed, then took herself off

to the kitchen to see whether Maggie wanted any jobs done.

The Bellamy farm was the last call on Mr Linwood's list. It was after four o'clock by the time he reached there.

Tom Bellamy was crossing the farmyard to the house when he rode in at the gate.

"I've really come to see your wife, Tom," Mr Linwood said, dismounting and tethering his horse.

"Then you'm out of luck, parson, 'cos she'm away to Kendal on a shop faddle. Still, she should be back afore long, so come you in. Kettle's on the boil."

"I just wanted to discuss the hymns for Sunday. She's deputising at the organ for Miss Hurst, who's visiting in Carlisle for the week."

Mr Linwood followed the farmer into the spotless kitchen and seated himself on a carved oak settle in the chimney corner. "And how are things with you?" he asked, as Bellamy removed the steaming kettle from the hob.

"Fair to middlin', thank'ee, parson. Fair to middlin'!"

"And your sons? Nothing wrong with them, I trust?"

"Nay! Best lads a man could have! Thanks be for it, I say. For it looks like there'll be just them an' me running t'place soon, way things is gooin'!"

Bellamy poured the water, hissing, into a brown crock teapot, and stirred it vigorously with a spoon.

"Why is that?"

"We conna keep labour, and that's a fact. Lost cowman yestiddy. Gone off wi' one o' they railway gangers, if you please!"

He poured the dark brew into two mugs, topped them up with thick creamy milk, and a generous helping of sugar.

Mr Linwood was shocked. "You surely don't mean young Daniels? I thought he'd settled with you?" He took the mug, and sipped the scalding tea.

Bellamy did likewise before replying gloomily: "Aye, and so did I! Treated 'im like one of us own, me and t'missus did, arter his feyther died." He sighed heavily. "Ah'd planned a bigger herd on account o' that lad!"

"But why should he give up a steady job with a good future to go and work on the railway?"

Bellamy scowled. "Railway pay seventeen shillin' a week, that's why! An' thee knaws, as well as I do, parson, I conna pay a man that wage."

Mr Linwood nodded. "True. But once the railway's finished, Tom . . . what then?"

Bellamy grunted. "Daft beggar thinks 'e'll mek enough in two three years to buy 'is own farm. So theer it is. *And*, that's not all!" He placed his mug down on the scrubbed kitchen table. "Henhouse were raided last neet! Missus lost all of a dozen of 'er best White Leg'orns. In a proper ole takin' she were about it!"

"Fox, was it?"

"Aye . . . a two-legged 'un!"

Through the open window came the sound of wheels rattling across the cobbled yard. Tom got up and went to the window. As he did so a voice called his name urgently: "Bellamy! Bellamy!"

" 'Tis Master Ralph! 'e's got missus wi' 'im an' all! Summat's up. I'd best go and see."

He went out and Mr Linwood followed, to find Ralph helping an hysterical Mrs Bellamy down from his wagonette.

"Whativver is it, mother?" Bellamy asked.

Sobs shook Mrs Bellamy's plump comfortable body.

"She's been robbed," Ralph said grimly. "I was driving along the lane when I saw her lying in the ditch, where the villain had pushed her having taken her purse, and a brooch, and – "

"Oh Tom . . . Tom . . . I thought 'e'd be th' death of me!" Mrs Bellamy wailed.

"Nay, 'tis past belief!" Bellamy was bewildered.

"You'd best come in and sit down, Mrs Bellamy," Mr Linwood said gently. "Tom's just brewed up. A cup of tea is what you need."

Rocking back and forth in her chair Mrs Bellamy told her story. "Carrier set me down as usual, at crossroads, and I'd just set off up th' lane when a man jumped out o' hedgebottom at me. I turned back – but it was too late – carrier 'ud gone."

"What sort of man was he, Mrs Bellamy?" asked Mr Linwood.

"A big swarthy-looking sort of chap, sir. More like a gipsy! Wi' a velveteen jacket an' a red plush weskit. He had a gold ring in one ear – I noticed it partikler, 'cos it sort of flashed as the sun caught it. He asked me for money, but I was that flummoxed I could say nowt! So he made a grab for me purse – an' when he found there was nobbut fifteen shillin' in it I . . . I thought he was goin' to hit me! He told me to hand over me brooch . . . an' . . . an' me weddin' ring! Then he ran off, giving me a shove, an' I fell back into ditch – where Mr Ralph found me!"

The poor soul burst into tears again at the recollection of her ordeal.

"By gom, if I get hands on th' varmint," cried Tom, doubling up his enormous fists, "I'll beat the daylight out of him, so I will! I'll not stand for it!"

"No more will I!" said Ralph harshly. "He can't have gone far. I'd say it's one of those navvies from the camp near Tebay! Get your lads, Bellamy! I'll round up some of the neighbours. We'll pay them a call."

"Surely, Ralph, it's a job for the magistrates," Mr Linwood began, but Ralph interrupted him roughly.

"We'll not wait for the law! It's time we had a reckoning with these people! We'll teach them a lesson they'll not forget!"

"Aye," Tom agreed grimly. He strode over to the rack of sporting guns on the wall beside the kitchen dresser, reached one down, and turned to his wife.

"Mother, you get young Jenny in to sit wi' you. I'm away to the twenty-acre to fetch the lads!"

In the navvies' encampment near Tebay, the "grog" or "tommy" shop was full of men drinking after a hard day's work. The atmosphere in the long wooden shack was thick with tobacco smoke. Behind a trestle table which served as a counter, the proprietor, Mick Malone, was having a spot of trouble with a surly ill-tempered character known as Patrick Varley.

Varley was a solitary sort. He worked, for the most part, in sullen silence, and spent his evenings drinking alone. This particular evening he had quickly drunk his pocket dry, but was demanding more beer on credit.

"Fill 'er up agen, I say," he growled, thrusting his pewter mug under Mick's nose.

"Gladly, Patrick," Mick replied equably. "But let's see the colour of your money first."

"Devil take ye for a money-grubbin' old skinflint! Haven't ye had all me week's pay already? And what I owed ye!"

Mick shrugged. "'Tis either cash or kind, so suit yerself."

This remark put Patrick into a proper rage. Dropping the mug he caught Mick by the shirt front pulling him half across the counter. "Aye, we know you and your little ways!" he growled. "Have the cloth off a man's back and sell it whilst it's still warm!"

Mick brushed Varley's hand away as if it had been a fly.

"Tell you what, Patrick," he said. "You can have as much beer as you can drink . . . in exchange for the shiny gold ring on y'r little finger. That's me offer – take it or leave it!"

Before Varley had time to answer, the door of the hut opened with a crash, and in strode Ralph Rawlings followed by a crowd of angry-looking farmers armed with cudgels, pitchforks, and other weapons.

The tommy shop was plunged into complete and utter silence for several moments. Mick Malone was the first to break it. "And what might ye be wantin' with the likes of us?" he demanded.

Ralph came straight to the point. "A woman was robbed of her purse, a brooch and her wedding ring at about four o'clock this afternoon. From the description she gave of her assailant, we've reason to believe he was a man from this camp!"

There were angry murmurs from the navvies, but Mick silenced them with a gesture.

"An' if so be it was someone from here an' ye find him . . . what do you propose to *do* with the villain, sir, if I might make so bold as to ask?"

The navvies sniggered and the farmers muttered angrily amongst themselves.

"What do I propose to do?" Ralph gave a switch to the riding crop he was carrying in one hand. "I'll tell you what I propose to do," he said. "I propose to flog him within an inch of his life!"

Several of the navvies sprang to their feet, but Mick held up a restraining hand. "'Tis bravely said," he began.

But Ralph went on. "Then I'll turn him over to the woman's husband and her sons. After that, *if* he survives, he'll be taken in front of the magistrates in Kendal, who will, no doubt, transport him for life!"

Mick laughed. "Well, now, lads," he cried. "You hear what the gentleman's proposing to do with one of ye. What are you going to do about it?"

That was all the navvies needed. With blood-curdling cries they launched themselves upon the farmers, and within seconds a battle royal was in progress.

Gerard had just finished his letter to Bella when he heard someone galloping towards the hut. Probably

Jake, he thought, coming back for something he'd forgotten. Then to his surprise he heard the Reverend Linwood's voice calling to him: "Gifford! Gifford! Are you there?"

He opened the door just as Mr Linwood drew level with the hut, and seeing him, reined in his horse. "Thank goodness I've found you! There's trouble brewing at the navvies' camp. A local farmer's wife was attacked this afternoon. There's little doubt it was one of your men!"

"I'm sorry," said Gerard. "What do you want me to do?"

"We'd best get over there! Ralph Rawlings found her, and he and her husband are out now raising the neighbourhood. They plan to raid the camp, and the mood they're in anything could happen! If only we could get there first, I might be able to reason with the farmers. Most of them are parishioners of mine."

"Just a minute!"

Gerard turned back into the hut and fetched Jake's shotgun, then got his horse. Five minutes later they were on the road to the navvies' camp, riding hard.

When they arrived, however, they knew by the noise coming from the tommy shop that they were too late.

Gerard thought for a moment. "There's a back entrance! Through a storeroom. Useless to go in by the front. We'd never make ourselves heard. We'll try shock tactics!"

They rode round to the back of the store and dismounted.

"I think you'd better stay here, sir," said Gerard.

But Mr Linwood wouldn't hear of it. "There are some of my parishioners in there," he said. "I have a duty to them!"

The storeroom door was unlocked. They went in and crossed to the door leading into the main room, where the fighting was. Kicking it open Gerard rushed in,

shouting at the top of his voice: "All right, you men! That's enough now!"

He might have been talking to the wind for all the

notice anyone took of him.

"It's no good, Gifford!" Mr Linwood shouted. "They'll never hear you!" He ducked as a wooden stool came flying through the air and crashed against the wall behind his head.

"Hold this," Gerard handed him the shotgun.

"What are you going to do?"

"I'll show you!"

With a leap, Gerard was on top of a table which had somehow managed to remain upright. "Give me the gun!"

"Is it loaded?" asked Mr Linwood, nervously.

"Just stand well back and keep still," said Gerard, and pointing at the ceiling, he fired. There was a shattering roar – and the battle ceased as if by magic.

Gerard felt weak at the knees. But taking a deep breath, he looked down at the sea of angry faces looking up at him, and said, "That's better! Now! What's the trouble?"

Mick Malone was again the first to speak. "Sure, Mr Gifford," he said suavely, "an' weren't we all enjoyin' ourselves in a properly peaceful manner, when this band of ruffians storms in without so much as a by your leave, and sets about the place!"

"That's a lie!" Tom Bellamy, jacket torn and an ugly gash on his forehead, pushed his way to the front. " 'Twas your lot started it!"

There were angry murmurs, but Mr Linwood stepped forward. "I've told Mr Gifford what happened to your wife, Tom, and why you are here." He looked around. "Where is Mr Rawlings?"

"If you're meanin' the high-toned gent with the riding whip – he sloped off a while back! Perhaps he had no stomach for the fight!"

The navvies jeered and catcalled in agreement.

"That's enough," shouted Gerard. And to his surprise they obeyed him.

"Mr Bellamy," he said, "have you seen anyone here who answers to your wife's description of the man who robbed her?"

"We'd no chance for a proper look. They started on us almost as soon as we stepped over threshold!"

A scuffle broke out near the entrance. One of the navvies had tried to slip out, but the farmers were too quick for him.

"Bring that man here," Gerard ordered. He was dragged forward, struggling and kicking, and shouting curses at his captors.

It was Patrick Varley. "Stop 'em, mates," he shouted. "It's a put up job! Gifford's on their side!"

Suddenly the room was in uproar again. But this time it was Mr Linwood who stopped them. "Be quiet, all of you!" he thundered. "Are you men . . . or animals! A man's wife has been robbed most brutally," he went on furiously. "Can you blame him for wanting to find the culprit?" He walked up to Varley. "If you're innocent, you've nothing to fear. Turn out your pockets!"

"I'll see you in Hades first!" Varley snarled.

There was a shocked silence for a moment. Then Mr Linwood said lightly, "Well, my man, there is no doubt that some of us will get there sooner than others!"

A few of the navvies tittered at this, and the farmers joined in. Gerard, who was now standing beside Mr Linwood, ordered Varley to do as he had been told, and to empty his pockets. But before the man could move, Tom Bellamy burst out: "Nay. Hold on! Let's see that ring!"

He grabbed Varley's grimy fist and held it up. "My wife's wedding ring, you villain!" he roared.

" 'Tis boughten!" cried Varley, his face suddenly shiny with sweat. "I bought it in Kendal yesterday!"

"Can you prove it, Mr Bellamy?" asked Gerard.

"Aye, I can that. It 'as 'er initials, as well as mine, an' the date we was wed, engraved inside it!"

"Take it off, Varley," Gerard ordered.

"I'm takin' no orders from a boy what's still wet behind the ears!" Varley replied. "It takes a man to give orders! You want the ring . . . you'll have to get it off!"

The room was suddenly very still.

Gerard looked at Varley, and saw a man toughened and brutalised by years of hard physical labour, with fists like sledgehammers, and shoulders used to shifting the weight of twenty tons of muck a day. Jake Joynson's warning came back to him. He swallowed the feeling of panic rising in his throat, and took a step forward.

"Patrick Varley!" Mick Malone's voice sounded more like a caress than a threat. "Will ye stop makin' a bigger fool of yourself than ye are already? Let's see the inside of that ring, now, and what about the contents of y'r pockets? Come on! Give the moths a treat!"

There was a roar of laughter, and Bellamy, seizing his opportunity, wrenched the ring from Varley's finger. He handed it to Gerard. "It's hers all right, sir. See for yourself."

Gerard looked at the engraving then handed it back. "Right," he said to Varley, "and now you empty your pockets!"

With an oath, Varley complied, tossing a heap of miscellaneous objects on the floor.

"There's her brooch," said Tom Bellamy, with satisfaction. "Aye, and her purse!"

He bent down, and picking them up, slipped the brooch into his pocket. Then he opened the purse.

"Theer's five shillin' 'ere," he said. "Theer was another 'alf sovereign when she left Kendal!"

"Was there now," Mick looked in the purse then at Varley. "Then ye're a cheat as well as a liar! For when ye paid me the half sovereign ye owed me this evenin', ye said ye was broke! An' to think I believed ye, an' was nearly moved to generosity."

"Well, that's proof enough for any magistrate," said Bellamy. "We'll be takin' 'im along, Mr Gifford!"

"No, Mr Bellamy!"

"Eh? What's that?"

"I said no! He's an employee of the Company, and as their representative, I will be responsible for handing him over to the magistrates in the morning!"

"Nay, I'll not 'ave that." Bellamy was beginning to get angry again. "What's to prevent 'im escapin' in the meantime?"

"He won't. You have my word. Mr Malone!"

"Yes, Mr Gifford?"

"You've keys to both doors of the storeroom, I take it?"

"I have!"

"Then I'd be obliged if you would see that Varley is confined there until I come for him tomorrow morning!"

"It will be a pleasure, sir!" Mick believed in keeping on good terms with both sides of an argument as far as he could.

"That's settled then," said Mr Linwood. "You and I, Tom, will meet at the vicarage tomorrow morning, then accompany Mr Gifford to Kendal!"

After a moment's hesitation, Bellamy agreed.

"Now," Mr Linwood went on, "get home to your good wife, Tom. She'll be anxious for the sight of you. And that goes for all of you!" he said, addressing the rest of the farmers.

Sheepishly they left the building, and after a moment or two, Gerard and Mr Linwood followed. Out in the night air Gerard gave a long sigh of relief.

"You did well, my boy," Mr Linwood said warmly. "Very well indeed!"

"Did I? To tell the truth, sir . . . I was scared half to death!"

"Well you managed to conceal it admirably. I do not think you will have much trouble in your dealings with the navvies in future!"

Gerard was sceptical. "That remains to be seen," he said. "But I am glad I took Jake's advice!"

"And who is Jake, pray?"

"Mr Brassey's head overseer. He told me –" Gerard broke off in astonishment. "But here he is!"

Jake came riding through the row of huts as if the devil and all his fiends were after him.

"Best get back to the depot, Mr Gifford!" he shouted. "The timber store's on fire!"

Chapter six

By the time Gerard, and Mr Linwood, together with Jake and as many of the navvies as they could muster, got back to the depot, the timber store was ablaze from end to end, and the flames, fanned by the wind, were spreading to the adjoining wagon shed.

"Get a bucket chain going, Jake!" Gerard shouted, and made for his office to rescue his papers.

"Right!" Jake ordered the men to follow him and set off at a run towards the huge wooden tanks which supplied the depot with its water.

"What can I do to help?" Mr Linwood called after Gerard.

"Get the horses out of the stables! A couple of men will assist you!"

He raced into the hut, seized his valise, and emptying out his personal belongings on to the floor, began cramming papers into it.

"Mr Gifford!" He recognised the voice of one of the gangers, and went to the door.

"What is it?"

"Wind's changing direction! See!"

Gerard looked to where the man was pointing. "The powder store!"

"Aye! Fire's heading straight for it!"

"Tell Jake! If that gunpowder goes up – everything else goes up with it!"

Gerard began to run towards the shed where the barrels of gunpowder were stored. He was almost there when an explosion ripped the air, throwing him to the ground.

As he staggered to his feet, Jake came up followed by four of the gangers. "What was that, Jake?"

"The paraffin store!"

He turned. Where the paraffin store had stood, there was nothing now but a wall of flame, a billowing cloud of black, acrid smoke. Beyond, and further to the right, silhouetted starkly against the lurid glow of burning buildings, he saw men carrying water.

"How long before the fire brigade gets here?"

"Your guess is as good as mine! I sent for them before coming for you!"

"We've got to get those barrels out!"

He ran towards the shed, taking the key of the padlock out of his pocket. He unlocked it, and with Jake's help, thrust aside the heavy timber beam barring the door, and swung it open. The gangers rushed forward to begin unloading the barrels from the wagon, but Gerard stopped them.

"There isn't time! It'll be quicker to push the wagon out!"

He knocked the brake off, and they began pushing, trying desperately to move the heavily-laden vehicle. But it would not budge an inch.

"Come on! Get it moving!" Jake roared, exhorting the men to further effort. "Altogether now! Push!"

They pushed until Gerard thought his lungs would burst, but still it would not move.

There was a sudden loud crash above their heads, and one of the men let out a yell: "The roof's ablaze!"

A burning baulk of timber fell in a shower of sparks, and without thinking, Gerard went to push it away from the barrels of gunpowder. It caught the back of his hand in one sickening, searing second, and he cried out with the pain of it.

"Mr Gifford!" Jake came towards him. "Are you all right?"

Furious with himself, Gerard shouted angrily, "Of course I am! Come on, now! Get this wagon moving!"

They made a last, almost superhuman effort, and

finally, they heard the massive wheels begin to creak, then turn. "She's going!" Gerard shouted.

Slowly the wheels gathered momentum. With renewed strength, they fairly trundled the wagon out of the building and on to the narrow strip of land which separated them from the burning buildings. By dint of two pushing at the back, and four pulling on the shafts, they managed to reach the top of an embankment which sloped steeply down to a stream beneath. With a mighty shove, they pushed the wagon over the edge. As it plummeted down, crashing between the rocks, Jake yelled: "Down! Everybody down!"

There was a shattering, deafening roar, as the gunpowder exploded, throwing up a shower of rocks and soil and other debris which cascaded down around the men lying on the ground.

"Jake! Jake!" Gerard shifted his weight and raised himself on an elbow, to look across at Jake's recumbent form. With a grunt, Jake sat up and peered glumly around.

"Fifty barrels of gunpowder gone up in smoke!" he complained bitterly.

But Gerard could have laughed out loud with relief at finding him unharmed. "What do fifty barrels of gunpowder matter? We could have lost the entire depot, and our lives too! But back to work – there's still the fire to deal with!"

A ragged cheer came from the weary men still carrying buckets of water to the burning sheds. A bell clanged in the distance. "The fire brigade," Gerard shouted.

"Not before time!" Jake scrambled to his feet. "And it's beginning to rain!" he said. "That's summat to be cheerful about, onny road!"

"Gerard!" Gerard turned to see Bella running towards him, hatless, her hair streaming behind her, her face as white as a ghost. For a moment, he thought she *was* a ghost, her appearance was so wild and unexpected.

"Where's Papa? Where *is* he?" In her anxiety she clutched his injured hand, and he almost shouted with the pain. Before he could answer Jake stepped up to her.

"The Reverend's all right, miss," he said. "The last I saw of him, he was taking the horses out of harm's way! He's safe enough, never fear!"

Thankfully she turned to Gerard. "Tom Bellamy told us father was coming here, and when we saw the glow of the fire we got the trap and came to look for him."

"We?" Gerard felt the ground slowly beginning to slide away beneath him.

"Maggie and me. We heard the explosion! It was terrifying! Gerard? What is it? What's the matter?"

But Gerard was beyond answering. Everying was spining round faster, and faster. He felt the ground rise up to meet him, and pitched forward into merciful oblivion.

When next he opened his eyes, it was broad daylight, and he was lying in a white-painted, low-ceilinged bedroom, furnished sparsely with one or two old-fashioned pieces of oak furniture. He sat up, but the movement caused a sudden stab of pain in his right hand, and looking down, he saw it had been bandaged most professionally. The events of the previous night came flooding back to him, and he climbed out of bed. He must get back to the depot as quickly as possible. But where were his clothes? He sank down feeling weak and dizzy, and was just pondering what to do next, when there was a tap at the door, and Mr Linwood came in.

"Ah, my boy," he said cheerily. "So you are awake at last! How is the hand? Is it giving you much pain?"

"No, sir, not much," said Gerard. "I take it I am the recipient of your hospitality once more."

Mr Linwood smiled. "You came most unwillingly: After you had recovered consciousness – in the trap, half-way home – you kept on insisting that you must return to the depot. But Bella took no notice – and I must say she was quite right! Doctor Graham said it was a nasty burn that you had sustained, though no permanent injury would ensue – but he, too, would not hear of you going anywhere, but to bed. He is calling this morning to renew the dressing. Do you feel well enough to come down to breakfast?"

"Yes, sir! But I cannot find my clothes."

"Of course!" Mr Linwood laughed. "They were in such a state, Maggie took them away and has done the best she can to make them more presentable again. I'll send them up. Do not hurry, breakfast will wait for you!"

Half an hour later, still shaky, but feeling much better, Gerard went downstairs and joined Mr Linwood and Bella in the morning room. Over breakfast, they discussed the fire, and Bella told him that the rain, which had come on heavily, combined with the efforts of the fire brigade, had put the fire out much more quickly than had seemed possible.

"By the time we had packed you into the trap, Gerard," she went on, "and found papa, who had taken the horses to a nearby farm for safety, the worst was over. And the news this morning is that all is safe now, and there is no danger of the fire starting again!"

"All the same," Gerard said. "I must be away back to the depot as soon as possible. There will be a great deal to do, clearing the debris, checking the stock, and making out requisitions for new buildings."

"You cannot go before Doctor Graham sees you." Bella sounded very determined.

"I *must*, Bella! The work cannot be held up to fuss over a mere burn."

"Fuss!" Bella's blue eyes sparkled angrily as she got up from the table. "Of all the ungrateful wretches! Well, you must do as you please. But you will get no sympathy from me if it takes bad ways. It will be your own fault." With that she stalked from the room, shutting the door behind her with a decided bang.

Gerard was stunned.

Mr Linwood chuckled. "There is no need to look so devastated, my boy!" he said. "She is, after all, only concerned about your welfare. She will have forgotten all about it in a few minutes. But for the sake of peace and quiet, you had better wait and see the doctor."

Mr Linwood was right. When Doctor Graham called a little while later, Bella brought him in, chattering merrily away as if nothing had happened.

Gerard decided he would never understand the reasonings of the feminine mind, but nevertheless, he was glad that he was evidently back in her good graces again.

Doctor Graham renewed the dressing, remarking that he thought they had met before, but could not remember the circumstances. When Mr Linwood reminded him of the night they had called him out to the stranded coach on Shap Fell, he chuckled and asked Gerard whether he deliberately courted trouble, or whether it followed naturally in his wake?

They were all surprised at Gerard's serious reaction to what had been a light-hearted question. "It would take too long, sir, to relate to you the events which have occurred over the last few weeks, but I am coming to the opinion that there is some . . . unnatural . . . element at work, with the destruction of the railway as its objective."

Bella was shocked. "You cannot mean that somebody started the fire last night deliberately?"

"I do not know, Bella. That is why I am anxious to get back to the depot before the men begin clearing up. They may destroy any clues as to how the fire started!"

"But you cannot ride! How can you hold the reins with your hand a mass of bandages?"

"That is easily solved." Doctor Graham smiled at Gerard. "I will drive you there, in the gig. I have to go in that direction in any case, so you will not be inconveniencing me in the least."

"And I," said Mr Linwood, rising from his chair, "I will ride after you with Tom Bellamy. You've not forgotten our appoinment with the magistrate in Kendal, Gerard?"

Gerard was startled. The fire had pushed everything else out of his mind. He had completely forgotten Patrick Varley and the events at the tommy shop! There was so much to do. He suddenly felt overwhelmed by it all. As if sensing his indecision, Mr Linwood went on: "Perhaps we could relieve you of the man Varley? I assure you he is not likely to escape Tom Bellamy's clutches! We could take him into Kendal in the wagonette, hand him over to the magistrate, and do whatever is necessary to prefer charges against him, leaving you free to go straight to the depot."

Thanking Providence for having put him in the way of such helpful friends, Gerard agreed. "But Malone will need a note," he suggested, "authorising him to hand Varley over to you!"

Bella jumped up. "I'll write it," she began, and then stopped in surprise.

From the hall came the sound of scuffling, and screams of rage. Then Maggie's voice raised in wrath.

"Stop it, you little varmint! Stop it this instant!"

The door opened, and Maggie entered, tugging at the squirming figure of a small child.

"Bless my soul, Maggie!" cried Mr Linwood. "What is going on?"

"You may well ask!" gasped Maggie, giving a final tug which brought the child round to face the astonished company. "In my henhouse, she was! A-stealin' of the eggs! Caught her in the act!"

Mr Linwood looked at the culprit, who had now subsided into sobs, which shook her small frame convulsively. She could not have been more than nine or ten years of age, and resembled nothing so much as a piece of flotsam dredged up on the beach after high tide.

Underneath a grubby apron a narrow shift of coarse grey sacking covered her thin body, her legs and feet were bare and mottled blue with cold. Her face was hidden beneath a mop of tangled black hair, and a pair of grimy hands covered her eyes.

"What is your name, child?" Mr Linwood asked gently. "And where are you from?"

The answer came with a gulp and a sniff. "Tissie!"

Mr Linwood turned to the others in bewilderment. "What does she say?"

"Tishy or Tissie, or some such outlandish name!" Doctor Graham replied. "By the looks of her, I'd say she's from the navvies' camp. There are a score or more of them running wild around there. All in varying stages of neglect and filth."

"Doctor! Please!" Bella protested.

Doctor Graham shrugged. "It is perfectly true. Little more than savages, some of them, from what I've seen!"

"How can you let her hear you talk so!" Bella crossed over, and stooping, tried to prise the grubby hands apart so that she might see the child's face.

"Don't be frightened," she said. "No harm can come to you here!"

The fingers of one hand opened slightly, and a tearful eye regarded her thoughtfully. Bella smiled encouragingly, and after a moment, Tissie's hands descended to clutch at her apron which she immediately applied to her face with a scrubbing motion. The dirt, however, was too ingrained to respond to this treatment. But her eyes, as she looked up at Bella, were blue as a summer sky.

"Come," Bella said, and drawing the child over to the sofa, she sat down and placed an arm around her. "Now, tell us your name again!"

"Tissie!" The answer came more confidently this time.

"Well, Tissie. Is there no food at home that you should rob Maggie's hens?"

"None since Monday," was the reply, "'cos 'e's in debt

to the tommy shop, an' they won't gie us no more credit!"

Bella looked across at Gerard. "What does she mean?" she demanded.

Gerard knew only too well what the child meant, but not how to explain a system which he himself had to uphold, though he hated and detested it.

"Well you see, Bella," he began, "the Company pays the navvies monthly. And because, in the main, they are working across country, and maybe miles from any village or town where they could purchase food, and other necessities, a 'tommy shop' is set up on the site. The word 'tommy' is a slang term used for such provisions. The trouble is, in many cases, a navvy will drink his whole month's pay in one week, and then, until the next pay day, he and his family have to live on credit."

"But that means, surely, that his next month's pay is already taken to pay off the debt?"

"Exactly!" barked Doctor Graham. "It is an invidious system. In some cases, money never changes hands. The men receive tickets in lieu of wages, and since they can only exchange those tickets in the tommy shops, the shop owners can charge what they like for their products. Though he half kills himself with extra work the navvy can never be free from debt!"

"I have never heard of anything so monstrous," Bella's eyes blazed at Gerard accusingly.

"It has always been so," Gerard said helplessly. "The men prefer it that way. And the sub-contractors use it as a means to keep the men bound to them! In known cases of hardship, Mr Brassey helps out, with a gift of food or money. But it's not always possible to find out where help is most needed."

"But something, surely, could be done to protect the women and children from the results of the men's excesses?" Bella turned to Tissie. "Do you not go to school, child?"

"What's school, miss?"

"You must know what school is! A place where you go to learn to read . . . and write . . . and to do sums!"

Tissie shook her head.

"Then what do you do all day?"

"Laik about, mostly. An' run errands for me mam!" Her face brightened, and she continued eagerly. "I'se good at fetchin' beer for th'men! Nivver a drop spilled, though the ground be ever so rough!"

"Would you go to school, if there was one?"

"Dunno, miss!"

"Mr Brassey plans to open a school for the children at Shap. And a chapel, too," Gerard said hopefully.

"Yes, I had heard about the chapel. Very commendable!" Mr Linwood frowned. "The trouble with the school, though, will be finding a suitable teacher!" He paused and continued wryly. "By the glint in her eye, I rather fancy we'd have Bella applying for the job. But it would not do, Bella. Teaching village children is one thing – but children like these are completely outside your experience. You would not know how to deal with them."

"You think not?" Bella began, but Tissie interrupted her.

"*Would* you teach us, miss?"

Bella looked down at the grimy tear-stained face upturned to hers. "Would you like that, Tissie?"

"Aye, miss!"

"Why, I wonder?"

" 'Cos you'm pretty . . . an' . . . an' smell nice . . . an' wear pretty clothes." Timidly she stroked the sleeve of Bella's flowered muslin gown.

Bella stood up, casting a triumphant, excited glance at her father. "Thank you, Tissie," she said, and held out her hand. "We'll go along with Maggie now, shall we, and see what we can find for your breakfast!"

"Aye, an' after that, it'll be the tub for thee, my lass!" said Maggie firmly. "We'll send thee 'ome a sight cleaner, or my name's not Maggie Henderson!"

As the door closed behind them, Mr Linwood heaved a sigh.

"Something tells me, Gerard," he said, "that I am in for a thoroughly uncomfortable time with this headstrong daughter of mine!"

Gerard smiled, but forbore comment. A little while later, he and Doctor Graham left for the depot at Tebay.

Chapter seven

"How long is it going to take to get things straight, Jake?" Gerard asked later that morning, as he and Jake finished their tour of the depot.

A pall of smoke still hung in the air, and ash from burnt timber lay thickly on the ground. The timber store and paraffin shed were completely gutted, and several stacks of railway sleepers had also gone up in flames. But the navvies were already working away at clearing the debris, and the sound of hammering and sawing announced the fact that the carpenters had set about repairing the less seriously damaged huts.

It could be worse, I suppose, Gerard told himself. But not much.

Jake, however, was more optimistic. "Four or five days from now, we'll be back to normal, I reckon," he prophesied briskly. And Gerard felt slightly comforted.

As they made their way to his office, which had mercifully escaped the fire, Gerard asked Jake if he had any idea as to how it could have started.

Jake looked grim: "I believe it were done deliberate!" He went on to state his reasons. "I found a can of axle grease and a pile of oily rags behind what's left of the timber shed this morning. I'm certain sure they weren't there last night when I did my rounds before leaving! And there's another thing."

He fished in the pocket of his corduroy trousers, and brought out a small metal object which he handed to Gerard. "One of the lads found this, in the rubble of the paraffin shed."

Gerard took it from him and looked at it. It was a small round medallion of some kind, blackened and disfigured by the heat. He rubbed it between his thumb and forefinger, and was rewarded with a reddish gleam. Could it be gold? He looked closer, and saw faint traces of an engraving on one side. He was reminded of a gold seal which Mr Locke wore on his watch chain. He had seen him seal letters and documents with it scores of times and had often admired it.

"You'd better leave it with me, Jake," he said, slipping it into his breast pocket for safety. "I'll clean it up, and study it a bit more. It's not much to go on, but it's better than nothing. At the moment, anyway, we've more urgent things to attend to."

The morning sped by as they set about ordering replacements for lost stores, and estimating the cost of the damage for insurance purposes. At twelve o'clock Gerard threw down his pen and announced that he must get some fresh air. Jake readily agreed, and suggested that they ride out to Helter Waste, an area of peat bog some few miles away, across which it was proposed to route the line.

"We've got a problem on our hands there," he said.

Gerard looked at him. "Only there, Jake?"

Jake stared back, and then the irony of his remark struck him, and they both laughed.

It was a relief to leave the mess and confusion of the depot behind. Out in the open country, riding across springy moorland turf under a clear sky, and with the sound of larks high above, Gerard felt his spirits begin to lift. They stopped at an inn for a lunch of bread and cheese and home brewed ale. While they ate, Gerard questioned Jake about Helter Waste and the difficulties involved in laying a line across it.

"Hast ever heard of Chat Moss, Mr Gifford?" Jake asked. "On the Liverpool to Manchester line?"

"Yes, indeed!" Gerard cut himself another slice of the sharp Lancashire cheese, and reached for the butter. The bread was new baked and crusty, and he bit into it with relish. "As a matter of fact, Mr Locke worked on it as assistant engineer to Mr Stephenson. But that was more than fifteen years ago!"

"Aye, quite that! Tough grass on the top, it was. Thirty or so feet of soggy soil, then clay and quicksand!" Jake took a swig at his ale, and gave a chuckle. "Local farmers used to put wooden pattens on their cows' hooves in case they strayed into it."

"You're joking, surely?" The idea of cows with clogs on was irrestibly comic.

"True as I'm a-sittin' here!" Jake glanced ruefully at his empty mug, and Gerard called to the landlord to fill it up again.

"How did they get the line across then?"

"They made rafts of hurdles, branches of trees, and heather and such. Laid 'em down so they overlapped, then tipped layers of sand and gravel, soil and cinders, on top of them. As they sank into the bog, so more layers were piled on top, until in the end they reached bottom and made a solid foundation to lay the rails across. Simple, when you think on it!"

"And it will work at Helter Waste?"

"Aye. It's a smaller area to deal with, which makes it easier. And there's plenty of scrub, heather, gorse and such, to use. As for sand and gravel, well, there'll be no trouble there. Mr Brassey has interests in one of the local gravel pits, I'm told."

Gerard wondered if there was anything Mr Brassey did not have an interest in when it came to building railways! But time was pressing, and if they were to get to Helter Waste and back before nightfall, they must be on their way.

An hour's hard riding brought them to their destination. It was a lonely place, and the peat bog was clearly visible between tufts of coarse brown grass interspersed with the bright green of spagnum moss.

They dismounted and surveyed the scene. "Put up a

few grouse here, I shouldn't wonder," observed Jake.

Gerard thought curlews the more likely, and congratulated himself a few minutes later, when he heard a plaintive bubbling cry, and a curlew winged its way into the sky. For some reason it made him think of Bella.

They tethered their horses to a bush by the roadside, and ventured into the moss, water oozing up around their feet. It seemed incredible to Gerard that anyone should try to put heavy iron rails on top of a such a surface, and even more incredible to think they could drive a train across it! For nearly an hour they traversed the ground back and forth discussing the best way of tackling the job. The air was fresh and clean, and Gerard felt a thousand miles away from the depot and all its problems.

At last, however, they finished what they had to do, and returned to their horses. Gerard was just preparing to mount when he heard the sound of a cart coming along the road, some distance away. He turned and saw a pony trap travelling at breakneck speed, swaying from side to side. A girl was standing up in the driver's seat pulling on the reins, while a smaller figure beside her clung to the side of the trap screaming in terror.

To his horror, he recognised the girl as Bella. "It's Miss Linwood," he cried. "We must stop them. They'll never make that bend!"

They jumped on their horses and reached the corner just a few seconds before the trap. As it came alongside, Jake made a grab for the pony's head. The shock nearly tore his arms from their sockets, but he held on grimly, and between running, and being dragged along, he finally brought pony and trap to a halt.

Bella sank down on to her seat, gathering the frantic Tissie into her arms.

"It's all right now, Tissie!" she said, vainly trying to calm the child. "It's all over. You are safe!"

"What on earth are you doing so far from home?"

Gerard demanded. "And what made the pony bolt?"

She took a deep breath in an effort to control herself. "It . . . it was some boys, throwing stones. At the navvies' camp. I was taking Tissie home. I . . . I should have waited for Papa. Maggie wanted me to!"

Tissie's sobs were quieter now, but she clung to Bella like a limpet, her small body still shaking with fright.

Gerard took off his jacket, and they wrapped it around her, then set off for the camp.

It seemed strangely quiet when they arrived. There were no children to be seen, and the doors of the huts were all closed. Though no human face appeared at any of the windows, Gerard had the feeling that they were being watched. When they stopped in front of the shack where Tissie lived, he told Jake to remain outside to guard the horses and trap.

Bella insisted on going in with him. And, sensing that it would be useless to argue, he took Tissie by the hand and went inside.

The sour smell of dirt, and grease and fetid air, which met him, made his stomach turn, and he wondered how Bella would react. He heard her give a horrified gasp, and hoped fervently she would not faint. But she advanced into the room with firm steps, and stood looking about her in undisguised amazement.

It was a long room dimly lit by two small windows. Down either side beds were ranged against the walls, one on top of the other, like bunks on a ship. There must have been at least twenty of them. In the centre a table, roughly made of two planks nailed together set upon trestles, held a collection of battered tin plates, mugs, and spoons. A half-eaten loaf lay alongside a piece of grey looking cheese, and Bella noted, with a shudder, the imprint of grimy fingers on the loaf.

A few wooden stools lay scattered about in confusion as if they had been kicked aside in a hurry. And from the rafters in the ceiling there hung suspended a most

extraordinary contraption. It resembled nothing so much as an enormous wooden cage with a trap-door in the bottom. It was empty, but Bella wondered what sort of a creature it could be intended for.

Tissie ran towards a door at the far end of the room, calling, "Mam! It's me!"

The door opened, and a woman stood there, with an infant clutching at her skirt. Her hair hung about her face in wisps, and she wore a sleazy grey bodice, held together at the front with a rusty pin. A drab woollen skirt, and a pair of down-at-heel slippers completed her dress. Her whole appearance was one of abject poverty and defeat. She listened to Tissie's tale with a dull, listless air, never once glancing at Bella and Gerard, who stood in a state of acute embarrassment, not knowing whether to go or stay.

When Tissie had finished, however, and paused for breath, she drew the child to her, and looked at them timidly.

"I'm right sorry she's give you so much trouble," she said. Hearing her voice, Bella realised with a shock that she must be quite young.

"She was no trouble," Bella assured her. "And I hope you won't mind, but we . . . there are some things for you in the trap!" She turned to Gerard, and he went out to fetch them. While he was gone, Bella tried to engage the woman in conversation, but somehow the right words wouldn't come, and she was relieved when Gerard reappeared carrying the basket of food which Maggie had insisted on sending. They placed it on the trestle table, and the woman watched, expressionless, as they unpacked the butter, eggs, cheese, and other things it contained. When it was empty, and they prepared to leave, she still said nothing, but Tissie ran forward, and flinging her arms round Bella, gave her such a hug that it was all she could do to restrain her tears.

"We must go," she implored Gerard, and almost ran

from the room. Pausing only to lay some coins on the table, all he had with him, he followed. Subdued and silent, they climbed into the trap. Gerard gathered up the reins.

"I'll drive Miss Linwood home, Jake," he said. "You go on back to the depot. I'll not be long."

As they reached the end of the row of huts, Bella looked back. But the door of Tissie's hut was firmly closed. She pulled the collar of her jacket up against her throat. She felt cold, and tired, and very sad.

"Perhaps now, Bella, you will have learnt your lesson, and will believe me when I say that these people are completely beyond the comprehension of ordinary decent God-fearing folk like ourselves!"

"Papa! It is not like you to be so hard!" Bella looked at her father in shocked dismay. Still shaken from her experience at the camp, she had turned to him for comfort and understanding. She found his uncompromising attitude very hard to bear.

"I do not wish to appear hard, my dear," Mr Linwood replied, "but they are not like us. They have no moral standards whatsoever. Most of them, so I am led to believe, do not even acknowledge the existence of a Divine Providence!"

"Can you blame them?"

"Bella!"

She looked round the room in which they were sitting, with its cheerful fire and comfortable furniture.

"The animals on Tom Bellamy's farm are better housed and fed than are the navvies' families! It is true, Papa! The hut Tissie lives in is nothing but a broken-down shack. She, her mother and father, and five other children, share it with a score or more lodgers! And I swear it is no bigger than our stable, where we house but three horses! Surely that cannot be right!"

"No, my dear, but you must realise –"

But Bella would not let him finish. "The children sleep in an enormous wooden cage which hangs from the ceiling. In order to go to bed, they have to climb up a ladder, which is taken away once they are inside. And there they stay until someone remembers to bring the ladder for them to come down in the morning!"

Mr Linwood laid down his pipe. "Is this really so?"

"Yes! Gerard told me on the way home. I thought it was a cage for some animal . . . or bird! I would not believe him at first."

"But supposing there should be a fire?"

"Then they would perish before they could be rescued! For the mother is a poor shiftless creature, and the father never there, spending all his spare time in the tommy shop drinking with his cronies!"

Mr Linwood was silent. Bella got up and knelt on the rug by his chair. "Papa!" she pleaded. "Surely it cannot be right for women and children to live in such misery? Can you not . . . can *we* not do something about it?"

Mr Linwood shook his head helplessly. "They are the responsibility of the railway company, my child. You heard Gerard say how Mr Brassey does the best he can for them. But you must believe me when I tell you that they do not want to be helped! This is the way they choose to live. They would not thank you for trying to alter it."

"But the children, Papa! They have no choice! And what future have they? Must they be condemned to this wandering, nomadic sort of existence? Surely they are entitled to be given a chance to lead a better life? That is only fair."

"Bella, Bella!" Mr Linwood protested. "Your feelings do you credit. But feelings are not enough. One must be practical about such matters. I hear the railway company is appointing a chaplain once the laying of the line is under way. I shall, of course, make myself known to him, and ascertain whether I can be of any assistance."

"But *I* want to help, too! There must be something I can do!"

Mr Linwood looked down at his daughter's eager face, and sighed. There had been a time, too, when he had wanted to set the world to rights. Now he was getting old, and set in his ways, content to jog along comfortably in the little world which God had ordained for his ministry. Perhaps he had been too comfortable of late. As he pondered, there came a knock at the door and Maggie came in with a letter.

"It's for you, Miss Bella," she said. "From the depot. The lad's waiting for an answer."

Bella took the letter and opened it. "It's from Gerard! But he's not been gone more than an hour!" She began to read.

"Not more trouble?" Mr Linwood asked, anxiously.

Bella looked up, her face radiant. "No, Papa! He says that when he got back, he found his employer, Mr Locke, arrived from London. Parliament has passed the Act authorising the railway!"

"Well, well, that is good news!"

"And he says . . . oh, Papa, listen! 'The Ceremony of the cutting of the first sod will take place shortly at Birkbeck, where there will be a brass band in attendance, sundry jollifications for the workpeople, and a cold collation for the official guests!" Bella looked across at her father, and laughed. "But there's more," she went on. "The ceremony will be performed by Mr Cornelius Nicholson, the mayor of Kendal, and I shall be delighted if you and your father will do me the honour of being my guests on this occasion!"

The letter fell from her hand. "Oh, Papa! How wonderful!"

"You think we should go?" Mr Linwood teased her.

"But of course! It will be an historic occasion! I shall wear my new bonnet. The one with the cerise ribbons."

"I see. And whom do you propose to captivate with that? I assure you, there is no need to go to such lengths for Gerard. He is quite captivated already!"

"What nonsense!" Bella rose to her feet. "I'll write and say we'll be pleased to accept." She went over to her writing desk, but paused before sitting down.

"Papa?"

"Yes, my dear?"

She looked thoughtfully at him.

"Do you suppose Gerard will introduce us to his famous Mr Brassey?"

Chapter eight

On a bright clear July morning, in the year 1844, a great crowd of people gathered at Birkbeck, just north of Tebay, to watch the ceremony of the cutting of the first sod.

Bella and her father were early arrivals on the scene, which was as colourful and lively as a holiday fair. Stalls had been set up for the sale of sweetmeats and refreshments, and everybody had turned up in their Sunday best in honour of the occasion.

"It seems as if half Westmorland is here, Papa!" Bella exclaimed.

"Cumberland, too." Mr Linwood pointed to a carriage with yellow wheels, in which two gentlemen were sitting engrossed in conversation.

"Goodness! Lord Lonsdale and the Bishop of Carlisle." Bella was impressed.

"God and Mammon well represented, eh, my dear?" Mr Linwood went on. "Of course, Lord Lonsdale is a shareholder of the company, or so I am told."

But Bella was not listening. She was scanning the crowd for one particular face.

"I do think Gerard might have been here to meet us," she said presently. "After all, we are his guests!"

"I've no doubt he'll join us as soon as he can. In all probability he has to wait upon his employers before seeking us out."

"Yes, of course." Bella brightened up at this, and the next moment exclaimed in surprise: "Look who is here!"

Ralph Rawlings was making his way towards them through the crowd. He saluted them with an ironic bow.

"Well, Bella, I suppose you know your bonnet is the envy of every other female? Your servant, Uncle!"

Mr Linwood returned his bow. "We hardly expected to see you, Ralph," he said, "knowing your views on the railway."

Ralph shrugged. "I was out riding this way, and thought I might meet one or two friends. And you, sir? Not often you take a holiday from parish affairs."

"Oh, but we are official guests," Bella said proudly.

"Really? Of whom?"

"Of Mr Gifford. You met at the vicarage last winter, the night of the blizzard! Don't you remember?"

"Oh yes." The corners of Ralph's mouth turned down disagreeably. "Some sort of clerk wasn't he?"

Bella eyed him frostily. "Mr Gifford is an assistant surveyor, working personally with Mr Locke, the Resident Engineer of the line!"

"Is he, indeed? Well, he can be the Grand Panjandrum as far as I am concerned. Personally, I thought him a rather pompous young prig!"

"And you, cousin, are an insufferable snob!" Bella fairly blazed with anger.

"I think I see Gerard approaching," Mr Linwood intervened hastily.

"In that case I will take my leave." Ralph turned to go. "Do not let him see you scowling so, Bella. It makes you look positively plain!" With that parting shot he disappeared into the crowd leaving Bella, for once, speechless.

When Gerard came up, out of breath, and full of apologies, he thought at first that she was angry with him. But she quickly recovered her high spirits, and demanded that he take them to see the navvies.

"They are over there, at the edge of the field. One of them has a concertina, and they seem to be enjoying themselves immensely!"

There must have been nearly a hundred navvies gathered round a small open space a little apart from the rest of the crowd. Some were sitting on the ground listening to the music, others were wrestling, juggling with beer mugs, and indulging in various other forms of horseplay. When the concertina broke into the lively rhythm of a jig, however, the open space was quickly filled with an eager throng of dancers, heel-and toe-ing it with a gusto that set the watchers stamping and clapping their hands in time.

Bella was fascinated by the clothes they wore. "Just look at that man's waistcoat! Sky blue sateen with gilt buttons! You have nothing nearly so fine, Papa!"

She was looking at a giant of a man, who was leaping and whirling with enormous energy. He wore a pair of moleskin trousers, and a square-tailed velveteen jacket. A gaudy neckerchief and the sky blue waistcoat completed his attire. His face was crimson with exertion, and his hair, a mass of tight black curls, glistened with perspiration. He was dancing as if his very life depended upon it, his comrades cheering him on.

Bella found her own feet beginning to tap out the rhythm. "Who is he, Gerard?" she asked.

"They call him Brandy Jack!"

"On account of his insobriety, I presume?" Mr Linwood sounded disapproving.

"There's a little more to it than that, sir! He worked on the Rouen to Le Havre line in France. Brandy was as cheap there as beer is here. And his workmates are grown heartily sick of hearing him talk about it, hence the nickname!"

"He must be as strong as an ox!"

"Indeed he is!" Gerard laughed. "The other day I saw him carrying home his dinner from Kendal market."

"What is so extraordinary in that?" Bella wanted to know.

"He had bought himself the whole carcass of a young bullock, and was trudging back to his lodging with the beast slung around his neck and shoulders, wearing it as easily as I might wear a cravat!"

While they were still laughing at the comic picture Gerard conjured up, Bella saw Brandy Jack leave the dance and approach her, one hand outstretched, and a broad smile upon his face.

"Beggin' y'r pardon for being' so bold, ma'am," he said, "but would you care to take a turn at the dance?"

Bella blushed crimson and Mr Linwood looked daggers at the man. Gerard explained hurriedly that there was no time, as the ceremony would no doubt begin very soon. And at that very moment, the brass band struck up with *Here the Conquering Hero Comes*, heralding the arrival of Mr Nicholson.

"Sure, an' wouldn't that be just my luck!" said Brandy Jack, ruefully. "Own to it now, ma'am, weren't you just longing to be in there footin' it wi' th' rest of us?"

Bella admitted she was, and would have engaged the man in further conversation, but Mr Linwood drew her away.

"Can you imagine, Bella," he said severely, when they were safely out of earshot, "can you imagine what people would have said if you had been seen dancing with a *navvy*?"

To his consternation, and Gerard's amusement, Bella sighed regretfully. "No, Papa, I cannot! But it would have been fun to find out!"

Turning to Gerard, she asked if the great Mr Brassey had put in an appearance as yet. On Gerard admitting that he had, she smiled sweetly at him. "You are going to introduce us to him, aren't you Gerard?"

"Bella!" Mr Linwood's sense of the proprieties had received a second blow.

Looking from one to the other of them, Bella's face alive with determination and mischief, and her father's, stiff with disapproval, Gerard decided that diplomacy was called for.

He addressed his reply to Mr Linwood. "Sir, I meant to tell you, but the navvies distracted us! Mr Brassey is very grateful for the assistance you have given me over the past months. He will be delighted if you will join him after the ceremony."

He turned to Bella. "Shall we go?" he said. "It would be a pity to miss the ceremony after all!"

She said nothing, but gave him a curt little nod. They went to join the rest of the official party.

The ceremony was over. Mr Nicholson had performed his part admirably, and all the appropriate speeches had been spoken. Now, in the marquee set apart for them, the directors and shareholders of the new Lancaster to Carlisle Railway were entertaining their guests. A liberal cold buffet had been provided, and the scene was an animated one.

Bella knew a great many of the people there, but since the vicarage at Elmden was remote, did not normally meet them from one year's end to another. She went gaily from group to group, catching up on all the latest news, and thoroughly enjoying herself. But her eyes kept straying to the long buffet table, where her father and Gerard were deep in conversation with two or three other gentlemen. When Gerard left them and came towards her, she realised, with a tremor of excitement, that her great moment had come.

"Mr Brassey would like to meet you, Bella," he said. When Mr Brassey broke off his conversation to greet her, however, she did not know what to say.

Gerard, sensing her shyness, came to her aid. "I have been telling Miss Linwood about your plan for a school at Shap, sir!"

"And what does Miss Linwood think of the idea?" Mr Brassey smiled at her.

"I think naught but good can come of it, sir!" Bella replied. "I have seen how some of the children are forced to live." She stopped, but then went on hastily, "That is, I know that in some cases it cannot be helped, and my father says it is how the parents would wish to live. But the children should be given a chance to . . . to . . . " She stopped again in confusion, and her father took up the conversation.

"My daughter's enthusiasm is inclined to run away with her at times, Mr Brassey. Nevertheless, she is very much concerned for the welfare of the navvies' children."

"Obviously! Very gratifying in one so young, and if I may say so, so charming!"

Mr Brassey beamed and Bella decided to venture further.

"I would like my concern to take a *practical* form, Mr Brassey – if that were possible!"

Mr Linwood shook his head.

But Mr Brassey was amused. "Do I take it you are offering your services as a teacher?" he asked.

"I would like it more than anything!"

"Sir!" Mr Linwood looked sternly at Bella. "I have already told my daughter that she is far too young and inexperienced for such a post. I trust you will pardon her presumption!"

"Oh, but you are right . . . quite right, sir!" Mr Brassey said hastily. Then he went on, "Yet I feel sure you would consider letting her assist the teacher on occasion? He will, in all probability, be the chaplain of the line, and though his scholarly qualifications will be beyond reproach, I hardly think he will be able to instruct the girls in such feminine accomplishments as sewing and knitting, for example."

"I could certainly do that, sir!" Bella cried eagerly. "My father will vouch for my proficiency in such homely crafts, though he may not readily do so for my academic qualities."

Mr Brassey chuckled. "You possess one quality at any rate, young lady, which is essential for any teacher!"

"And what is that?"

"Determination! You may depend upon it, when the

school at Shap opens its doors, I'll not forget you!"

That promise was good enough for Bella. She spent the rest of the day in a positive haze of happiness. When, finally, she and her father departed for home, she declared that it had been the most wonderful day of her whole life.

A statement which Gerard echoed with all his heart.

He was not only glad for Bella. He felt that at last the railway would go through. Now the Company could get on with the job of building it.

The evening of that same day, a meeting took place between Ralph Rawlings and Nathan Raphael, in a private room of an inn in Kendal. Ralph was in an uneasy state of mind. The affair of the man Varley, and the raid on the navvies' camp had not turned out as he had expected, owing to Gerard's firm handling of the situation. Now that the line had the official sanction of Parliament it would be more difficult to drum up opposition to it. He mentally cursed the day he had put his signature to the I.O.U. of Eskdale's, and he heartily disliked the seedy little man who was his Lordship's messenger.

Mr Raphael was, as usual, taking snuff – an occupation which he pursued with dedicated concentration.

After a deal of sniffling, snuffling, and trumpeting into a dubious-looking handkerchief, he leered at Ralph, and remarked that His Lordship was naturally most distressed to hear of the shocking fire at the railway depot at Tebay.

"I am sure he was!" Ralph replied sarcastically, and was rewarded with a brief lopsided grin.

"However," the little man went on, "we gather that the depot is already again in full working order. The question is, Mr Rawlings, what do you propose to do now to ensure that the line does not reach Carlisle – at least not before the East Coast Route reaches Newcastle!"

"Newcastle? Why Newcastle? I thought Edinburgh was the main objective?"

"You are quite right. But since we last met there have been developments in the situation. Chief amongst these is the fact that costs have risen far more than we had allowed for. The line has already reached Berwick, as you probably know. But at this very moment, Mr Hudson is trying to persuade Sir Robert Peel and the Government to give him financial aid to carry on into Scotland. And he seems to be in a fair way to succeed in his endeavours. Should the West Coast route show signs of reaching Carlisle before we can get to Newcastle, however, the Government may well change their minds and offer financial aid to *that* project! You see our predicament?"

"I do, indeed. But I do not see what you can expect me to do – other than continued harassment of the work by local farmers and others who, like me, do not wish to see the railway line disrupting our countryside."

"These are delaying tactics, certainly, Mr Rawlings. But we do need more positive action!"

"Such as?"

"We leave it to your undoubted ingenuity, sir! Nothing immediate, perhaps. But a little later on, when the work has been in progress for a few weeks, we might contrive a little 'diversion' of some sort."

"Very well," said Ralph heatedly. "I am in no position to argue with His Lordship. But it will be difficult to find ways and means!"

"Oh come now, sir. The building of railways is, of necessity, a somewhat hazardous occupation! Earth embankments have been known to give way . . . tunnels cave in . . . even masonry can crumble and collapse seemingly without any logical explanation!"

Raphael crossed one leg over the other, and clasping his hands round his knees, rocked back and forth in rapt contemplation of the prospect. "Do you, by any chance, happen to have a list of the sub-contractors who will be employed in the building of bridges for the line?" he asked Ralph suddenly.

Ralph shook his head, remembering a certain notebook which he had 'acquired' one night, and lost again before he had had a chance of looking at it.

"A pity," mused Raphael. "But never mind. I believe I know such a man. He may be of use to us. I will give you his name presently."

Ralph hesitated, but could not resist asking: "About that I.O.U. of mine . . . ?

"Yes, Mr Rawlings?"

"I suppose you still have it . . . safe?"

Raphael smiled. "Oh yes, I assure you it is quite safe with me!"

"There is no chance . . . I mean . . . I had hoped that Eskdale . . . in view of the fact that I have already discharged part of our bargain . . . "

Raphael settled back more comfortably in his armchair before replying. He produced the inevitable snuff box once more, and then, tapping it, said, "No doubt, when His Lordship considers you have completely worked off your debt to him, he will order its destruction. But it is early days yet, Mr Rawlings. Early days!"

Chapter nine

For Gerard now, the days were not long enough for all that had to be done. From first light until dusk, and sometimes long after, he was at Brassey's beck and call, taking notes, writing memos, acting, as the great man himself put it, as his "good right hand". It was a novel experience for Gerard, and he found himself marvelling at the contractor's capacity for work, and his sheer genius for organisation. By the end of 1844, the first permanent rail had been laid on Shap Fell, and the line was employing close on four thousand men and over three hundred horses. For the Railway Company it was a race against time, a race to beat the East Coast route. And both Thomas Brassey and Joseph Locke were determined to win.

Sometimes Gerard and Brassey walked up and down the line, mile upon gruelling mile, in all weathers. The line was slowly beginning to take on the pattern of its eventual route. During these walks Gerard saw another side of the man. Brassey talked about the beautiful cities he had seen abroad, and the architecture of their fine buildings. He described his collection of sculpture and porcelain, of which he was a connoisseur. But always the conversation returned to his abiding passion, the building of railways. Whenever they stopped to inspect a cutting, a bridge, or even a simple culvert, he gave the job his complete attention, talking to the navvies, listening to their grievances, and often seeking their opinion of the work in hand. It was no wonder that the men respected him.

There was still a good deal of resentment against the railway, especially by the farmers. And the navvies did not help matters. On the day they received their monthly pay,

Kendal was like a town besieged. Shops closed, and people stayed indoors. For once the navvies had drunk their fill, and for some this meant spending almost an entire month's pay in a single day, the fighting began. They fought each other, and they fought any innocent bystander who happened to have the misfortune to get in their way.

One morning Brassey came to Gerard with an unusually gloomy face, waving a letter at him. "I must go back to London for a day or two, my boy. And I must leave immediately. But the dickens of it is that I've this meeting with the farmers at Claygate. You'll have to go in my place. It'll be the usual thing, I suppose. Complaints about crops being trampled, poaching . . ." He sighed. "I don't blame them. But what can we do, with only eight police for the whole line?"

"Sir! Have you seen the latest issue of the *Gazette*?"

"Not yet. Why?"

"They're calling for more lock-ups, special constables, and mounted police to prevent disturbances on pay days."

"Splendid!" Brassey's face broke into a broad grin. Then, seeing Gerard's look of surprise, he explained: "Let the townsfolk dig into their own pockets to protect their property. They make enough out of the Company by the trade we've brought them!"

"I hadn't looked at it like that," Gerard admitted. "But I do see what you mean. What time is the meeting, sir?"

"Two thirty!"

"Then, in that case would it be all right if I took Jake with me? We could call at Mossrigg on the way and see how the viaduct there is shaping?"

"Do that. And mind you tread warily with the farmers. We don't want to antagonise them any more than we have done already!"

Ragged storm clouds scudded across the sky as Gerard and Jake rode over to Mossrigg later that morning. A thin bitter wind scattered the remnants of the year's dried leaves across the road. The horses seemed nervous and ill at ease. As Gerard and Jake reined in beside a small beck to let them drink, a skein of geese fled south, honking their mournful cry.

"There's a change in the weather!" Jake said, watching them go. "'Appen we're in for a helm wind!"

"What's a helm wind?" Gerard wanted to know.

"'Tis a wicked bad 'un, they tell me. Blows from the east, across the Pennines. When it comes man and beast take cover!"

They mounted, and continued on their way, riding through a plantation of young fir trees, and out into a narrow wooded ravine with a stream tumbling through it. The viaduct, which would eventually straddle it, was a small one compared with the enormous structures to be built further north at Eamont and Lowther. But the main pillars were already in position, and the first graceful arch nearing completion.

A maze of scaffolding carried a light tramway across from one side to the other, and huge derricks, with blocks and pulleys, were hauling great chunks of stone into place. Men climbed over the scaffolding carrying planks and hods of mortar, whilst masons, perched aloft, chipped away at the stone as unconcerned as flies sunning themselves on a garden wall. The ringing cadence of hammer and chisel echoed back along the steep sides of the ravine. The trees and bushes, even the grass, were white with dust.

At the base of one of the pillars a group of men were busy mixing sand and lime, watched over by a stout individual who appeared to be laying down the law about something.

"Who's he, Jake?" Gerard asked, as they left their horses and made their way towards the group.

"Hindley, the sub-contractor."

"He seems to be in a bit of a taking about something!"

The argument, if indeed it was an argument, reached a climax just as Gerard and Jake drew near. The men

stopped working, and threw down their spades.

A positive bellow of rage shook Hindley. “Get back to work!” he yelled.

“Nay! We’ll not! Not till this is settled once for all!”

The workman who spoke, an elderly man, rubbed red-rimmed eyes with the back of his hand and turned to the others. "That's right, ain't it mates?"

There was a chorus of "Ayes", which served to infuriate Hindley even more.

"Do as you're told!" he roared. "Or I'll sack the lot of you!"

"What seems to be the trouble?" Gerard asked.

Hindley spun around. "And who might you be?"

Gerard explained, and Hindley listened with barely concealed impatience. Then when Gerard had finished he said: "Aye well. Ther't Brassey's chap, right? Well, I'm boss o' this job, and I'll take it kindly if thee'll not interfere wi' my workmen!"

"They may be your workmen," Gerard replied, "but the Company is paying you for the work they perform. And if they're not doing it, the Company is entitled to know why!"

There was a murmur of approval from the men, and the elderly man spoke up again.

" 'E keeps on at us to put more sand in the lime, sir! But 'e knows as well as we do that it's four o' sand to one o' lime! Otherwise the mortar'll be too dry!"

Hindley was just about to break into more abuse, when Jake, who had been thoughtfully poking at a clod of lime adhering to his boot, said: "Where d'you get y'r lime from, Mr Hindley?"

Taken aback, Hindley looked at Jake out of bloodshot eyes. "What's it to do wi' you?" he asked.

"Just wond'ring, that's all," said Jake mildly. "Looks a poor sort of colour to me!"

"What dost a' mean by that?" Hindley had stopped blustering, and was looking slightly uneasy. The workmen, relieved that his attention had been distracted from them, went quietly back to work. "Theer's nowt in my contract that says what sort o' lime I should use!"

Jake shrugged. "Aye, well, sorry I spoke, I'm sure."

He turned to Gerard. "Best be on our way, Mr Gifford!"

Hindley made as if to speak, then turned on his heel and walked away.

As they rode back up the ravine to the main road, Gerard asked Jake why he'd commented on the lime.

"Well, sir, Mr Brassey insists on a special kind of mortar for bridges and viaducts. And that calls for hydraulic lime, because it hardens under water."

"Isn't that what Hindley's using?"

"He may be. I could be wrong. But it looked cheap stuff to me!"

"Right! As soon as Mr Brassey gets back from London I'll bring him over to see for himself!"

"Aye. That'd be best, I reckon!"

Gerard gave his horse a nudge with his knee. "We'd better get a move on. I'm not looking forward to this meeting. I've a feeling there'll be trouble!"

Jake laughed. "Trouble's like physic, I always say. Swallow it quick, and it don't taste half so bad! Thinking about it's worst part."

They urged their horses into a gallop, and arrived at Claygate just before half-past two.

The first person Gerard saw when he entered the meeting room was Ralph Rawlings. They had not met since their encounter at Elmden Vicarage on the night of the blizzard over a year ago. Gerard wondered whether to speak to him, but Ralph merely gave him an indifferent glance, and went on talking to the man at his side. His presence, however, did nothing to boost Gerard's confidence.

The farmers were plainly in a hostile mood. Facing them, Gerard felt young and very inexperienced. He saw the anger in their faces, and sensed their resentment. Could he convince them that the railway was not an enemy, but a new, and as yet untried, friend?

He started off by apologising for Brassey's unavoidable

absence, and there was an immediate reaction from the back of the room.

"Shame on him! Sending an underling to do his dirty work!"

It was Ralph's voice. Gerard recognised it immediately, and felt the angry blood colour his cheeks.

"I am here to discuss problems," he replied, "not to exchange insults."

One or two of the farmers nodded their approval, but they were few among many. The complaints came thick and fast, and were always the same. How was the Company going to control the navvies with their wild ways?

Gerard explained Mr Brassey's plans for building a school and a chapel at Shap. There would be a chaplain in attendance full-time, so that the men could attend evening classes in reading, writing and arithmetic. This had already been tried out on other railway workings, and the result had been a great reduction in drunkenness and general misbehaviour.

"Most of the trouble the navvies cause stems from boredom and frustration," he went on. "In the main they are men from the cities, suddenly transplanted into an alien countryside with nothing to do after their day's work is finished. They do not have comfortable homes to go to, as you do. They live in overcrowded, temporary accommodation. Can you wonder that they fight among themselves, drink too much, and do things which men leading a normal life in secure, comfortable surroundings would never dream of doing?"

There was silence after he had finished speaking. And for a moment Gerard thought he had achieved a victory of sorts. But then Ralph Rawlings' voice rang out again. "Fine words! But what have they to do with us? We do not want your railway, or your navvies, spoiling our land, and disrupting our way of life. Down with the railways, I say!"

As if this was a prearranged signal, other voices took up the cry, and from all corners came the chant, "Down with the railways!" accompanied by the stamping of feet, whistles, and catcalls.

The room was suddenly in uproar.

Jake, who had been listening at the back, managed to struggle through to the raised dais on which Gerard was standing, trying to make himself heard above the din.

"Best give up, Mr Gifford," he shouted. "It's a put-up job. Somebody's out to wreck the meeting!"

"I know, Jake! And I've a good idea who it is!" Gerard jumped off the platform and pushed his way over to where Ralph Rawlings was standing surveying the confusion he had caused, a smile of malicious enjoyment on his face.

"Well, Mr Rawlings, we meet again!"

"Have we met before? I don't seem to remember the occasion!" Ralph replied. The commotion was beginning to die down, as the farmers turned to see what was going on.

Gerard laughed. "Surely you haven't forgotten the night of the blizzard? When we both had to seek shelter at Elmden Vicarage?"

Ralph shrugged. "It had escaped my memory!"

"But not mine, I assure you! For my coach had broken down on the road over Shap, and we would have been marooned there all night, maybe even for days, such are the hazards of travelling by *road* in winter!"

"Aye, 'tis true enough!" came a voice from behind him, and turning round, Gerard saw, to his surprise, the face of the young farmer who had been with him in the coach that night.

"If it 'adn't bin for 'im, an' parson," the farmer continued, "my missus might a' died, and the babby!" He went on to tell the events of that night, and finished up declaring that, as far as he was concerned, nothing would get him in a coach travelling over Shap again in winter.

"There'll be no need to take such risks," Gerard assured him, "once the railway's working."

It was said so quickly, the farmers were forced to laugh, and the meeting was resumed in a much more friendly atmosphere. There were no more interruptions, and when it closed Gerard felt he had at least made the farmers realise some of the problems the Company faced.

He did not see Ralph leave, but as he and Jake left the meeting, Jake remarked thoughtfully, "That Mr Rawlings, sir!"

"Yes, Jake. What about him?"

"Well, I can't swear to it, but I think I've seen him before!"

"It's more than likely. He lives near Tebay. At Meathrop Hall. You've probably seen him out riding somewhere!"

"Aye, I have that!" Jake looked grim. "If I'm not mistaken, and I don't think I am, it was him I saw riding up the lane from the depot on the night of the fire!"

"You didn't tell me!" Gerard was startled.

"No, to tell the truth it slipped me mind, what with one thing and another. But this afternoon I knew I'd seen him somewhere, and it suddenly dawned on me where it was. Curious, that!"

"Very curious!" Gerard fell to wondering just what Ralph's purpose had been in visiting the depot that night.

The weather had worsened during the course of the afternoon, and torrential rain had been added to the gale force wind.

On their way back, acting on an impulse, Gerard told Jake he intended taking another look at the viaduct.

"You needn't come if you're anxious to get back!" he said. But Jake indicated that he was in no hurry, and so, when they reached Mossrigg, they turned off into the ravine.

The wind tore down the valley after them with a hollow

booming sound, lashing the trees and bushes into a frenzy. The rain had swollen the little stream into a fury of foaming spray. When at last they reached the viaduct, they were astonished to find workmen still there.

Gerard asked why they had not gone home.

"Ask Hindley that!" said one, jerking his thumb in the direction of a nearby wooden shack. "We told 'im it were too dangerous up theer in this wind, but 'e said we 'ad to finish day's work, else we'd lose a day's pay!"

"We'll see about that!" Gerard knocked on the door of the hut, but there was no answer.

"Has anybody seen him lately?" he asked.

" 'E was in theer a while back. I seed 'im wi' me own eyes!" The man who spoke turned, and gave a sudden shout: "He's theer! Up yonder!"

Hindley was standing on top of one of the main pillars of the viaduct, just where the first arch began. When he saw them looking at him, he shook his fist and began shouting. But the wind carried his words away.

Gerard cupped his hands round his mouth and called, "Hindley! Come down!"

But he took no notice. He walked out along the parapet, across the first arch, and then appeared to bend down to look at the stonework. He straightened up, and as he did so a sudden gust of wind whipped him off his feet, and with a dreadful cry, he plunged down into the stream beneath.

They were stunned. One second the man had been there. The next . . . nothing.

Then there was a sound like distant thunder, and as Gerard still gazed in disbelief at the empty space where Hindley had been he saw the arch shudder and begin to break. The shock of it jerked him back to reality.

"Run! Run for your lives!" he shouted.

And they fled, as with a roar and a crash, the viaduct crumbled in ruins into the ravine.

Chapter ten

For several months after the collapse of the viaduct, work along the line proceeded smoothly, though with increased supervision and tighter control of the materials used by sub-contractors for their operations.

An inquest on Hindley had given a verdict of "Accidental Death", but there were those who reckoned he had deserved his fate. For the inquest Thomas Brassey held, on his return from London, proved beyond shadow of doubt, that his use of shoddy materials, and in particular, of sub-standard lime, had been the chief cause of the disaster.

By the summer of 1845, half the work on the line had been completed, and on Shap four-fifths of the cutting excavated. No less than five hundred men were at work on this, the most difficult operation along the whole length of the line!

Brassey had fulfilled his promise, and built both chapel and school high up on the fells overlooking the cutting. Close by were rows of huts, which the navvies had called after famous London thoroughfares. Painted on rough wooden boards, nailed to posts, were "Hanover Square", "Regent Street", and "The Strand". The first time Gerard came across them he laughed aloud, it was so unexpected seeing them there.

Sometimes he would get up at dawn, and climb the hillside behind the hut he shared with Jake to watch the light changing across the fells. He would listen to the curlews, and wonder what they made of the changing scene.

There were changes, too, at Elmden Vicarage. A new face was helping Maggie in the kitchen. A small, pert little face under a mop of black curls. A face that answered to the name of Tissie.

It had been Mr Linwood's idea. Maggie was getting older, and complaining more frequently of stiffness in her joints, and the "twinges" which came and went with the weather. Bella helped her as much as she was allowed to. But Maggie was an independent soul, and resented any interference in the domestic sphere in which she had reigned supreme for so long.

One day, at breakfast, Mr Linwood announced that he had found a solution to the problem. "Supposing she had someone young, someone inexperienced, to train and mould into her ways? Someone like Tissie, for example?"

Bella was thrilled. "You mean she could come and live here? What a marvellous idea! I could give her lessons."

"Yes, why not? In her spare time, of course."

So it was decided. And the arrangement proved very successful. As Mr Linwood had surmised, Maggie enjoyed having someone young and biddable to order about and "mother". And Bella found Tissie a stimulating pupil, quick, and eager to learn.

Yet Bella was still far from content with her lot. Though she heard from Gerard at regular intervals, he was seldom able to visit her at the vicarage owing to the pressure of work. Her heart was still firmly set on teaching the children at Shap school, but as yet, Mr Brassey's promised summons had not come. It was very frustrating and there were days when she found it difficult to conceal her longing to escape from the routine of vicarage life.

Bella was delighted, therefore, when her father suggested driving over to Shap to see how the work on the cutting was progressing. He also offered to take Tissie with them so that she could visit her mother. Tissie's parents had "moved up" the line, and were now living in one of the huts there.

When they had delivered Tissie, Bella and her father

walked across to the edge of the cutting. It was an astonishing sight. It looked as if a giant had taken an enormous bite out of the hillside. For a quarter of a mile earth and rock had been dug out to a depth of sixty feet, driving a great gap between the fells which towered on

either side. At the bottom of the cutting men, tiny, like ants, were scurrying about, pushing and pulling barrows of earth, while larger ants, horses, pulled wagon loads of stone and timber along a single line track.

They were so fascinated by the scene they did not see

Gerard approaching until he was almost upon them. He and Jake had been inspecting one of the culverts at the top of the cutting which was intended to take flood water away from the site. With the recent heavy rains and an exceptionally bad storm the previous night, the level of the water in the culvert had risen by three inches or more, and there was danger of flooding.

"I am not surprised," Mr Linwood observed. "I have never known so much rain as we've had this past week. Last night was simply appalling. The Kent overflowed in Kendal, and I gather several families had to leave their homes!"

"What will you do about the culvert, Gerard?" Bella asked.

"We'll have to deepen it by at least six feet," Gerard replied. "And then line the sides with branches of trees and baulks of timber, to stop them giving away. The trouble is we're so short of men. We've lookouts posted on all the main roads, to catch men tramping from job to job. But there's a shortage of labour all over the country."

It was true. Everybody was building railways. According to *The Times*, the whole of England was in the grip of "Railway Fever"!

Seeing the worried look on Gerard's face, Bella sought to distract him.

"Have you a lodging up here, Gerard?" she asked.

"Yes. Over there." Gerard pointed to a small wooden building with a thatched roof, and a little iron chimney sticking out on one side.

"Jake and I share it," he went on, "and it combines dormitory, kitchen, living room, and office – all in one. It's a good thing we agree on most things – there's no room for argument!"

"May we see inside?" Bella asked.

"With pleasure, for I've something to show you! You too, sir, will find it fascinating, I'm sure." Gerard turned to Mr Linwood, who was still watching the work going on down below in the cutting.

Inside the hut Gerard picked up a bundle wrapped in sacking from among a clutter of things on the table which served as his desk. Unwrapping it, he withdrew a sword, which he handed to Mr Linwood.

"One of the men dug it up this morning," he said. "It was buried beneath a layer of peat, which I suppose is why it is in such good condition."

"It is indeed! Just look, Bella, how beautifully it is engraved. Silver, I should think!"

"I wonder who it could have belonged to?" Bella traced the pattern of leaves cunningly wrought on the hilt of the sword.

"Well, I have a theory about that." Gerard took the sword from her, running his fingers down the blade to where a rusty stain marked the smooth surface. "I think it's a relic of the '45 Rebellion!"

"Of course!" Mr Linwood exclaimed. "Left behind by one of Bonnie Prince Charlie's men on that ill-fated march on London. You could be right, my boy. In which case, it must be a hundred years old. Remarkable!"

Bella shivered. "It's sort of . . . ghostly, isn't it?" She went to the table, and stating that Gerard was even more untidy than her father, if that were possible, started energetically putting it to rights.

Gerard rewrapped the sword, and was looking for somewhere to put it, other than the table, when they heard the sound of a bugle, and men shouting, from below.

"Goodness!" Bella was startled. "What's that?"

"It's all right," Gerard assured her. "It's only a warning that they are about to blast some of the rock away in the cutting."

"I should like to see that," said Mr Linwood. "May we?"

"By all means!"

Gerard led them to a vantage point from which they could see down the whole length of the cutting.

"If we stand here," he said, "we should get a good view, but be out of range when the charge is fired. The shock waves sometimes produce unpleasant sensations."

In the cutting men were running for cover, and the horses were being led to safety. On the roads and tracks leading to and from the workings, red flags had been hoisted. Suddenly the commotion died down, and all was silent, except for the occasional call of a bird, and the far off sound of rushing water.

"What's happening now?" Bella's voice was almost a whisper.

"They are lighting the fuses," Gerard replied.

"How is the explosive laid?" Mr Linwood asked.

Gerard explained that first of all a hole was bored into the rock which the men wanted out of the way. Then a "stemmer" – an iron rod – was used to ram the gunpowder into the hole, and the hole sealed with clay. The fuse wire was then laid, and when all was ready, the warning bugle sounded and the men ran for cover. The match was applied to the fuse to ignite it, and that was it.

"It sounds simple enough," Mr Linwood observed. "But does anything ever go wrong?"

"Sometimes. If the stemmer, while ramming home the powder, strikes the rock, sparks fly off and ignite the powder before the man can get clear!"

"How horrible!" Bella shuddered.

"It doesn't often happen," Gerard said hurriedly, then went on: "Prepare yourself for a loud bang, Bella. The fuses should have been lit by now."

"Coo-ee! Miss Bella!"

Tissie's voice came clear as a bell from the other side of the cutting, and they saw her small figure running down the hillside towards them.

"Stay where you are! Don't move!" Gerard shouted. And at that moment the world around them shook with the sound of an explosion so violent it was like a physical blow. A cloud of dust enveloped them, and when it cleared, Tissie was nowhere to be seen.

"Where is she? What's happened to her?" cried Bella, in a panic.

"It's all right, my dear, I see her!" said Mr Linwood. "She's crossed over and is coming up the hill towards us."

A few minutes later Tissie joined them, dusty but triumphant, and scornful of Bella's scoldings as to the danger of not heeding blast warnings!

"We'm used to explosions, Miss Bella," she said, "living alongside the line. 'Tis safe enough if you know what you're about! I got a message for you, sir!" she concluded, handing Gerard a note.

"Who gave it to you, Tissie?" Gerard said, opening it.

"Nay, sir, I dunno who he was. Stopped me on t' road just now, and said to gie this paper to t' young gaffer. 'E gives us a penny!"

"Is anything wrong, Gerard?" Bella asked, noticing his frown.

"It's from one of the gangers further along the line, up Clifton way. He says the English and the Scots are planning a raid on the Irish navvies' camp, and he reckons there's going to be big trouble!"

"That bears out something the new chaplain, the Reverend Gillies, was saying to me only yesterday, Gerard!" Mr Linwood looked serious. "They are spoiling for a fight, I'm afraid!"

"I'd better go and talk to them – see if I can find out what their grievances are."

"You'll not go alone?" Bella pleaded. "At least take Jake with you!"

Gerard shook his head. "Jake's too much to do here. That culvert's got to be attended to. Besides, it's better I should go alone. It looks more unofficial."

"Gerard's right, Bella," said Mr Linwood. "Diplomacy is better than a show of force sometimes."

"I hardly think two men against a crowd is a show of force!" said Bella with some asperity, but she saw it was hopeless to press the matter further.

They went back to the hut. Jake had just arrived there, and after explaining the situation to him, Gerard took his leave.

After he had gone Bella and her father lingered awhile talking to Jake, and then, just as they were leaving, Bella came back to Jake. "There's something you can tell me, Jake," she said. "I picked up this seal earlier on this afternoon, when we were looking at the sword in Mr Gifford's office. I meant to ask him how he came by it."

"Oh, I can tell you that, miss. It was found among the rubble in the paraffin shed, the morning after the fire at the depot."

"You are quite sure?"

"Certain sure, miss! Chap as found it brought it straight to me. Mr Gifford's cleaned it up, I see, but I doubt he's had time to find out who it belongs to!"

Bella turned the seal over in the palm of her hand. "No, I don't suppose he has!"

Her father called impatiently: "Are you coming, Bella? It's getting late. Maggie will be wondering where we are!"

"I'm coming, Papa!" Bella slipped the seal into the pocket of her jacket, and, bidding Jake good afternoon, she hurried after her father and Tissie.

Jake watched her go. "Now that's a rum do," he muttered to himself. "I reckon as young miss there knows right well who owns that seal! But she's not telling!"

Chapter eleven

Later that evening it began to rain again, a steady downpour which quickly filled the ditches, and turned the churned up roads around Tebay into stretches of liquid mud.

Just as it was getting dark a servant at Meathrop Hall heard a frantic knocking at the door of the main entrance, and opening it, found Bella Linwood standing there.

Her light riding cloak enveloped her in dripping folds. Her hair hung in wet strands about her face.

"Is . . . is anything wrong, miss?" He stood aside to let her in, but Bella did not move.

"I want to see Master Ralph," she demanded.

The man was nonplussed. In his experience young ladies did not come calling at that time of night unaccompanied. And in such weather! He looked past her, expecting to see a companion, but the drive was empty save for her horse.

"He's not here, miss!"

"But I *must* see him! Where is he?" She sounded desperate.

"He mentioned something about Beresford's farm."

"On Shap Fell?"

"That's right, miss. Just beyond where they're making the cutting. Will you come in and —"

But she was away. He watched her go, bending low over the mare's neck, her slight figure merging with it, a blurred image of fleeting grace. Shaking his head, he shut the door. He wondered just what the young were coming to these days.

As the mare carried Bella towards Shap from Tebay, so Gerard was galloping towards it from the opposite direction.

The call to Clifton had been a hoax. He knew it as soon as he had arrived there, and found the place as quiet and orderly as a country churchyard. Someone had deliberately lured him away from the cutting. Why? For what reason? His mind ranged over the possibilities as he rode. He sensed trouble, and knew that he had found it immediately the cutting came into view. Above the pounding of his horse's hooves, and the swish and hiss of the rain he heard the noise of strife. In the semi-darkness of the workings, a pitched battle was in progress.

He jumped from his horse, and ran towards a milling crowd of angry navvies. In the centre of them towered the gigantic form of Brandy Jack – the navvy who had asked Bella to dance at the inauguration ceremony. As Gerard watched, helplessly, he saw him pluck a man bodily from amongst the struggling mass around him, hold him above his head for a moment, and then literally hurl him back into the crowd again. Another man detached himself from the battle, and ran towards Gerard shouting. It was Jake!

"It's no use, sir! They've gone crazy! There's no holding them!"

"What started it?"

"A rumour that the Scots were coming to raid the grog shop!"

"And were they!"

"Nay! I've seen no Scots. It was a trick to stop them working."

Gerard stared at him. "There was no trouble at Clifton either! So what's behind it?" A sudden thought came to him. "Have you finished the culvert?"

"Have I heck! Soon as they heard this rumpus start, the lads working with me downed tools and came to join the fray!"

"But I *told* you it was urgent! If this rain continues, and it overflows, it could cause a landslide. Why did you let them go?"

"Because there were six of them an' only one o' me!" Jake snapped. "An' last trump wouldn't have stopped 'em either! They've been boiling up to this for a week, and I can't say as I blame 'em. I reckon they're sick of working all hours God send, soaked to the skin, and living like pigs in a pen! And come to that, so am I!"

They glared at one another, tempers frayed to breaking point, and it was Gerard who finally broke the tension.

"Right!" he said. "I'll go and see what the score is. If, and I say 'if', you can get some help, come after me as fast as you can!"

Without waiting for an answer he got his horse, and mounting, rode off up the track leading to the culvert, leaving Jake staring after him.

High on the hillside overlooking the cutting, Ralph Rawlings was standing watching some half a dozen of his tenant farmers hauling a wagonload of muck and stones towards a point just above the culvert Jake and his men had been working on until the fighting had broken out.

The sound of the battle was like sweet music to his ears, for it meant that all was going well. Gifford had been called away by the false note. The navvies were too busy fighting to heed what was going on above their heads. If his plan succeeded, and even the weather seemed to be on his side, the railway line between Lancaster and Carlisle would be ruined once and for all. He would be free of his debt to Eskdale, and, he smiled grimly in the darkness, he would give himself the pleasure of dealing with Mr Nathan Raphael.

The wagon was heavy, and the ground wet and slippery with rain. Progress was slow, as the wheels tried to get a grip on the treacherous surface. Sweating and cursing, the men inched their way forward. He suspected that they were regretting their decision to help him, though they had been keen enough at the outset. They were all with him in their detestation of the railway.

At last the wagon was in place, poised above the culvert, and the men stopped to get their breath.

"Right," said Ralph after a minute or two. "Let's get on with it. You, Beresford, with Digby and Simes, get at the back ready to shove. The rest of you help me to guide it over the edge and into the culvert!"

The men began to murmur uneasily amongst themselves.

"Well? What are you waiting for? The sooner it's done, the quicker you'll be home and dry!"

Beresford, a big, slow-moving, blunt-speaking man, spoke up: "It's like this, sir. We don't like it. And that's a fact!"

"You don't like what?" Ralph slid his hand into the inside pocket of his greatcoat, and felt the small pistol nestling there.

"There's folk down there. In the cutting. Navvies they may be – but they're mortal men like us! If we block t'culvert and it overflows, we could start a landslide, and somebody might get killed!"

Ralph laughed. "I see! A belated attack of conscience, eh? But you knew what we were about. You agreed to do it. If you're so squeamish, one of you can go down now and warn them! Who will volunteer?"

Nobody moved, or spoke. Ralph laughed.

"Very well, then! Let's waste no more time. Get on with the job."

But Beresford stood his ground, doggedly. "Nay! I'll not do it! If thee wants it done, thee mun do it thy'sen! I'm off!"

He turned to go, and the others with him, but as he did so, Ralph shouted: "Stop! I'll put a bullet through the first man to leave!"

Beresford turned round slowly and faced him. The other men drew back, afraid.

"Thee'd best put that toy away, Master Ralph!"

Beresford said steadily. "We'm not your slaves! Thee cannot force us to do thy bidding!"

"Toy, is it?" Ralph's voice was high and unsteady. "We'll see!"

The sound of the shot, and Beresford's cry of pain rang out almost simultaneously.

"There's another pistol ready primed, should anyone else wish to argue with me!" said Ralph shakily.

Beresford lurched towards Ralph, clutching his shoulder, and at that moment they heard a horse approaching fast, and a girl's voice calling: "Ralph! Ralph! Where are you?"

"Bella!" Ralph looked round wildly, seeking somewhere to hide, but the farmers, as if the sound of her voice had released them from a spell, crowded round him, angry, menacing.

"What is it? What are you all doing here?" Bella cried, as she rode up.

She slipped from the saddle and stood looking at them. "I heard a shot! At least I thought it was! Was it a shot? Has there been an accident?"

"'Twere no accident, miss!" said one of the farmers. "'Tis Beresford. Master Ralph let fly at him!"

"Ralph?" Bella was bewildered. "Is he hurt?"

"I'm all right, Miss Bella," Beresford said gruffly, "'tis only a graze!"

"But what were you doing here? I *demand* to know!"

She listened as Beresford told her the reason for their presence, and what their intention had been.

"But there are men working down there!" she cried, when he had finished.

"Aye, miss!" said Beresford. "We didn't think of that at first. Master Ralph, 'e got us that worked up about t' railroad, and the harm it 'ud do us. All we thought about was tryin' to stop it! But we did change our minds, miss. Only 'e tried to make us go through wi' it! An' . . . an' when we wouldn't . . ." his voice trailed off into silence.

Bella looked across to where Ralph was standing, leaning against the wagon, his back towards them. "You had better go home, all of you!" she said. "Can you ride, Beresford?"

"Aye, miss, I'll manage!"

"Then go, before anyone else comes up here and starts asking questions!"

They went, silently. And when the sound of their horses had died away, she turned to Ralph.

"Are you out of your mind, Ralph?" she said. "Haven't you done enough damage already?"

"Bella! I warn you! Don't meddle in things which do not concern you!"

He strode towards her. "What are you doing here, anyway? How did you know where to find me?"

"Your man Gregory told me you had gone to Beresford's. I went there, and they sent me here!"

"Why? Why are you following me?"

"I wanted to give you something! This!" She held out her hand palm upwards.

"What is it?" He bent his head to look, and she drew back, closing her hand into a fist.

"It's the gold seal I gave you for your birthday! It was found in the rubble of the paraffin shed the morning after the fire at the railway depot at Tebay!"

"So!"

"Is that all you have to say? You started that fire, didn't you?"

He made no reply, and she went on: "People could have been killed if the gunpowder had not been moved in time!"

He laughed. "You are talking utter nonsense! Really, Bella, I think you should go home! The rain has addled your brain!"

"Don't lie to me, Ralph! You hated the railway from the very beginning! And you've done everything in your

power to stop it. But you've failed! And you'll go on failing, because you're wicked . . . evil . . . and Papa says evil will never triumph . . . never . . . never! And when I tell him –" She broke off with a gasp, as he gripped her wrist. "Let me go! You're hurting me!"

"Do you think I'd let you tell him?" Ralph demanded fiercely. "And if you did, do you think he'd believe you?"

"He . . . he would . . . if I showed him the seal!" she cried.

"But you won't, will you, cousin?" He tried to prise her fingers apart. "Because the seal is mine, and I intend to have it back!"

He twisted her wrist savagely, and she screamed with the pain.

"Let her go, Rawlings!" a voice called, and Gerard came rushing up to them. Ralph pushed Bella aside as Gerard grabbed him.

They rolled over and over towards the wagon, each desperately trying to get the upper hand. Floundering in the wet peat, they slipped and slithered to the edge of the culvert. At last Gerard managed to grab a fistful of Ralph's hair, and with a mighty heave, yanked him to his feet. As he did so, he saw the glint of metal in Ralph's right hand. Instinctively, he ducked. The pistol exploded with a noise that deafened him, but the shot whistled harmlessly past his head. He heard Bella scream: "Ralph! Take care! The bank!"

Straightening up, he saw Ralph's hands helplessly claw the air as the ground gave way beneath his feet, and he toppled slowly into the culvert. With a sickening lurch, the heavy wagon slid forward, and plunged in on top of him.

Horrified, Gerard stumbled across to Bella and helped her to her feet. She clung to him sobbing incoherently, and he tried to comfort her. After a little while, when she grew calmer, he led her away.

"There's nothing we can do now," he said. "It happened so quickly! He would not have known anything! Believe me, Bella!"

Chapter twelve

On the way home, Bella told Gerard of Ralph's attempt to fire the depot, and his plan to flood the cutting. "The disgrace will kill my aunt!" she cried bitterly. "As for Papa! I cannot bear it, Gerard!"

"There is no need for them to know why he died," Gerard assured her. "Only how it happened. The rain caused the bank to slip. It was as simple as that. All else will be a secret between us two!"

"But the farmers? Beresford and the others?"

"They have their own reason for keeping quiet. They'll not say a word for fear of implicating themselves!" To his relief this seemed to comfort her a little.

They arrived at the vicarage just as Mr Linwood was setting out to look for her. He heard their news in shocked silence, and leaving Bella in Maggie's care, hurried off to Meathrop Hall to break the news to Ralph's mother.

Gerard returned to Shap.

The rain, chief contributor to the night's disaster, had relented a little, and a fine soft drizzle had set in.

The navvies, having had their fill of fighting, were nursing their bruises, and obeyed meekly enough when ordered to help in the grisly task of recovering Ralph's body, and repairing the broken culvert.

All night long they worked, knee deep in water, digging out rocks and boulders, and lifting the broken parts of the wagon, until, in the grey light of morning, Ralph Rawlings' body was uncovered. Jake brought up an empty wagon, and they laid him on it, and covered him with a horse blanket one of the navvies had brought from somewhere.

Gerard gazed down at the grey shape and wondered, with a shiver, if this was how his father had looked when they found his body at Woodhead.

He was still standing there when they came from Meathrop Hall a little later, and took Ralph home.

The day of the funeral Elmdon church was packed with relatives, friends, and people from the estate. Gerard was late getting there, having been detained at the cutting. He slipped into an empty seat in one of the back pews, and looked around, wondering just how many of them had come out of curiosity.

At the inquest, the Coroner had passed a verdict of "Death by Misadventure", in the absence of any evidence as to how the accident had happened. But there had been a good deal of gossip as to what Ralph Rawlings had been doing that night, above the cutting, and in such weather.

Bella had not found it easy to keep their secret. But she and Gerard could only hope that, in time, speculation would die down and the whole affair be forgotten.

A muffled sneeze made Gerard start, and he glanced sidelong at the man sitting next to him. A seedy-looking individual, with a strong odour of snuff about him. Gerard wondered who he could be. He had certainly never seen the man before, and he looked out of place amongst the country folk seated around him. The Reverend Linwood began reading the "Burial of the Dead", and Gerard tried to concentrate on the service.

Later, however, in the churchyard, Gerard saw the man again, lurking in the shadow of a tall headstone. There was an air about him at once furtive yet defiant which filled Gerard with a vague sense of unease. As he watched, he saw him draw a piece of paper out of his pocket, study it briefly, then tear it into shreds. He held the pieces in the palm of his hand for a second, as if weighing them, and then dropped them at his feet. With the heel of his boot, he ground them into the wet clay. A movement at the graveside distracted Gerard's attention, and when he looked back again, the man had gone. He went across to join Bella and her father, noting as he did so, that the sun which had been struggling feebly all morning, was at last beginning to shine.

The trouble on the railway did not automatically cease after the tragedy at Shap cutting.

In February, 1846, despite Brassey's efforts to keep them apart, what amounted to a civil war erupted between the English and the Irish navvies at Penrith. The Westmorland Yeomanry had to be called out to stop the fighting. A few months later the navvies called a strike for higher wages and shorter working hours. But, by August, the line from Lancaster to Penrith was virtually complete.

Bella and Gerard saw little of one another during these months. As the work progressed, so Gerard's responsibilities grew, under Brassey's kindly but firm surveillance.

It seemed to Bella, when they did meet, that Gerard was preoccupied and more serious than when she had first known him. But then, she sensed a change in herself, too, now that she had Tissie to care for, and the girls from the navvies' camp coming to the vicarage twice a week for lessons. This last had been another of her father's ideas, readily agreed to by the chaplain of the school at Shap. The truth was that Bella could not yet bring herself to visit the place where Ralph had met his death. Maggie had grumbled at having what she called a "parcel of ragamuffins" invading the house. But it was not long before her motherly heart warmed to them, and she set about washing and mending their clothes, and contriving to replace those too worn to mend. And needless to say, no child ever went away from the vicarage hungry at the end of the morning!

One day in early October a letter arrived from Gerard which caused great excitement. As a rehearsal for a tour of inspection by the Directors of the Company, he was to take out the Company's locomotive *Centaur* on a trial run. And Bella, her father, and young Tissie, were all invited to accompany him!

Two days later they were waiting at Tebay when the *Centaur* puffed into view, smoke pouring from her tall smoke stack. Behind her she pulled two brand-new carriages, their side panels gleaming with varnish and gold paint, the windows sparkling bravely in the sun. With due ceremony Gerard handed them into the first carriage. They settled down on the crimson plush seats, and with a loud shriek from the steam whistle, they were off.

Soon they were rattling through open moorland at a spanking fifteen miles an hour. Mr Linwood appeared a trifle nervous when Gerard told him that this was the speed at which they were moving, but Tissie was in her element. Bouncing up and down with the motion of the train she demanded to know if they would be able to see the huts at Shap – and if so, could she wave to her mother from the open window?

"How long before we reach the cutting, Gerard?" Bella wanted to know.

"Not long. We are beginning to climb the incline now."

"Tell me, my boy," said Mr Linwood, "how will the engine contrive to pull several coaches at once up such a steep climb?"

"It will take on what is called a 'banking engine'," Gerard replied. "That is to say, another engine will be attached to the rear coach of the train to push it along, while the one in front is pulling."

"I imagine it will take a vast quantity of coal and

water, then?"

"It will depend on the size of the train, of course, sir. But for an average sized train about half a ton of coal and between seven and eight hundred gallons of water, I believe. We have not yet had the chance of proving this, of course."

"For such a short journey? Remarkable!"

"It's a steady climb— a gradient of one in seventy-five!"

"Ah well," Mr Linwood sighed, "it is all very strange and wonderful! And it will bring about many changes. All of them for the better, I hope!" He turned to contemplate the passing scene.

"Miss Bella! Look! I can see the cutting! And there's the huts, up on th' hill!" Tissie's nose was pressed against the window pane, and she was beside herself with excitement.

"Can I wave, miss? Can I open the window and wave? Please, miss, me mam might see me!"

"No, you cannot, Tissie! You might fall out . . . or . . . or get a cinder in your eye!"

"I won't, miss! Honest! Can I wave me hankie? *Please?*"

"Very well," said Bella with a sigh. "Mr Gifford will open the window for you, then. And I shall hold you firmly round your waist, just in case!"

Gerard let down the window, and Tissie hung out, flapping her handkerchief vigorously until the huts were no longer in sight. Then she sank back on to her seat with a sigh of satisfaction.

"I bet me mam did see me," she announced. "Our Tom 'ull be livid when 'e knows it was me!"

The engine gave a whistle as they reached the summit, and Gerard drew Bella to the window and they looked out. The stark rock face of the cutting loomed up before them on either side. Bella shivered slightly and whispered: "It seems like a dream now, that dreadful night when I stood up there and confronted Ralph! Sometimes it all seems like a dream. I don't think any of us ever really expected the railway to materialise."

"Well, it has!" Gerard grinned. "And by the middle of December the line will be officially open. Mr Locke has kept his promise to the shareholders. They didn't believe him when he said it could be done – but they'll have to eat their words now!"

"What's that you say, my boy?" Mr Linwood asked.

"I was just telling Bella that the line will be officially opened on December the fifteenth, sir!"

"Ah yes. I know, because I have received an invitation to the official opening from Mr Gillies, the Chaplain. I am to travel by train from Lancaster with him to Penrith, where another train from Carlisle will meet us, carrying some three hundred guests."

"Yes, I believe that is the plan," Gerard laughed. "Then, I gather, both trains will proceed to Carlisle, where they will be greeted by the band of the Yeomanry Cavalry, and, of course, a great gathering of spectators!"

"And I," said Bella, sitting down again. "I shall ride up on to the fells to watch them go by! If Papa can spare a thought from hobnobbing with the high and mighty – he may wave to me in passing. And you, Gerard, if you've a mind to, may even prevail upon the driver of the train to salute me on the steam whistle!"

"I may very well do that," Gerard assured her. "And now we must look out for Lowther Castle. We shall be passing near by shortly!"

"Where will you go when the line is finished, Gerard?" Bella asked a little later on.

"To Scotland, to work on the next section of the line."

"And will you always be . . . travelling on . . . from one job to another?"

"I suppose so. You see, Bella, this is only the beginning. This line, and many others like it, will be the main arteries of communication, with tributaries carrying people and goods wherever they need to go. Soon you will think as little of travelling to London as to Kendal market. Mr Brassey even dreams of building a railway tunnel beneath the English Channel!"

They laughed at the notion. But for the rest of the journey Bella was strangely quiet.

When they reached Penrith Gerard ordered a carriage to take them back to Tebay by road. Mr Linwood thanked him warmly for the expedition. "I declare I shall become quite addicted to rail travel," he said. "And I shall positively enjoy the Diocesan Conference in Carlisle now that there is no risk of spending the night in a snow drift on Shap!"

Gerard laughed, thinking of their first meeting, but Bella was not so enthusiastic.

"It is all very new and exciting, Gerard! But you cannot seriously expect me to prefer a snorting iron monster to my darling Maria! Besides, her four swift feet can take me to places where your engines will never go."

Tissie came dancing up with a posy in her hand. "It's for you, sir!" she told Gerard. "'Tis for your buttonhole. 'Twas a grand ride, sir! I liked it fine!"

Gerard helped her into the carriage, and stood watching them as they drove away. Was it only just over three years since he had first met Bella and her father? He could not seem to remember a time when they were not there bringing warmth and affection into his life.

He walked back across the track to where *Centaur* was standing, surrounded by an inquisitive crowd. Jake was standing on the footplate, and joining him he was soon lost in discussion about the performance of the engine on its trial run.

Two months later on a brilliant clear, cold December morning Bella rode up over the fells to Shap Summit. She sat looking at the sweep of the hills stretching as far as the eye could see, majestic in their loneliness.

A keen wind ruffled her hair, and on it was borne the sound of a distant approaching train. Then another sound impinged itself upon her ear, and she turned to see Gerard riding towards her. She was astonished, for she expected him to be on the train with her father and all the official guests to the opening of the line.

"Why are you not on the train?" she asked. "With all the other important people."

"Because I wanted to be here with you. I shall not be missed in all that throng. And Mr Brassey gave me leave of absence."

They heard the train whistle in the distance, and then a curlew's bubbling cry.

"How strange! Strange to hear that sound up here, where once I heard only the curlew, and the wind blowing across the fells!"

Bella looked across at Gerard. "I suppose the curlew will get used to it," she said. "And so shall I."

"Bella!" Gerard reached forward and took her hand. "Bella, will you still write to me when I am in Scotland?"

"Of course I will! I'll always write to you wherever you are. I promise, Gerard!"

The train came in sight, puffing up the incline, and now they could see the people hanging out of the windows, and the crowded open carriages at the back.

"I am so very glad I came to this beautiful north country of yours, Bella," Gerard said. "See the smoke drifting over Shap? It will take me away quite soon now, but one day it will bring me back. It will always bring me back. That I promise, Bella!"

From the train came the sound of cheering, and as it passed the passengers waved. They watched until it disappeared into the cutting, and then they turned their horses and rode slowly away together.

Fact and Fiction

More than a century ago navvies, using nothing but picks and shovels, and horse-drawn wagons, built the seventy miles of the Lancaster to Carlisle Railway in just under two and a half years, at a cost of £1,200,000. Now, the northern section of the M6 motorway runs parallel with it – built by men using the most modern machinery in the world. It took them considerably longer, and cost in the region of £60,000,000.

Today it takes five hours to get from London to Glasgow by rail. In 1838 the quickest way was by train to Liverpool, then by boat to Ardrossan – a fourteen-hour sea journey – and finally another train to Glasgow. But by 1840 the railway had leapfrogged forward as far as Lancaster. The next leap, however, was to prove the most difficult. Between Lancaster and Carlisle lay the mountains and fells, the rivers and valleys of what is now called Cumbria.

The two top railway engineers of the day, George Stephenson and Joseph Locke, had very different ideas as to the route the line should take. In the end Joseph Locke's plan to take it up and over Shap Fell was adopted. He gave the contract for the work to Thomas Brassey – the "king" of the railway contractors, and it was the beginning of a partnership which was to take them all over the world, building railways. Brassey employed a total of 10,000 navvies, English, Irish, and Scots, on the Lancaster to Carlisle Railway, and *Smoke Over Shap* is the story of the navvies and their impact on the lives of those who came into contact with them.

The other main characters in the book, Gerard,